THE
BILLIONAIRE'S

THE INTERN TRILOGY BOOK 3

PROMISE

paige press

THE
BILLIONAIRE'S
THE INTERN TRILOGY BOOK 3
PROMISE

lia hunt

Paige Press
Leander, TX 78641

Ebook:
ISBN: 978-1-953520-67-8

Print:
ISBN: 978-1-953520-78-4

CHAPTER ONE

EMERY

IT'S IMPOSSIBLE.

Absolutely, totally, completely impossible.

I'm in some kind of bizarre dream, or maybe I passed out on my OB/GYN's desk at the sight of those foot stirrups or something. Maybe the sight of these pure white walls filled with images of smiling pregnant women has done something to my brain. I have seen the pregnant women, and I've somehow *become* the pregnant women.

But it can't be real.

Because it is just not possible for me to be pregnant.

After all, I'm responsible. I grew up in Kansas with a mother who loved and cared about me, who taught me right from wrong, who raised me on a farm so that I know how to milk a cow, ride a horse, and enter a chicken coop and emerge with all of my fingers intact.

On. A. Farm.

Meaning, I know how things work, okay?

Mom even managed to have an only semi-awkward conversation about the birds and the bees with me. She told me about protection. She even showed me which aisle to buy them in, and then we never, ever talked about it again.

But I knew! And I researched because I love a good research moment. So when I knew that losing my virginity was imminent it's not as if I was so innocent that I didn't understand the importance of using a condom every time. And we did. We did!

The first time and all the many, many times after that, Harrison wore a condom. Even when I didn't want to wait the extra ten seconds, even when I'd probably have just taken a chance because all I wanted was his bare cock inside of me, he still put one on. In his penthouse, the office, or at the barn at my house back in Kansas. We always, always wore a condom.

Even when the sight of him hard and throbbing in front of me made me tempted to ask him to go without, to just pull out at the critical moment, we never did that. He always stopped and put on protection.

And when I decided the temptation to tempt fate was too great, that we might slip up, I came to the OB/GYN for birth control so that this exact situation wouldn't happen.

I'd made so many plans for the after-party of my birth control. Hell, I was even considering going to a sex shop! I was thinking candy-flavored lube and nipple pasties and whatever else they sold in a sex shop.

I wasn't expecting this.

Because it's not possible.

"But that's not possible," I say the words out loud, sure airing them will fix this. My voice sounds about four octaves higher than it should be, possibly because I've had the wind knocked out of me by this completely outlandish error. Because that's what it is. An error. Is she even looking at my file? She probably walked into the wrong room. So many vaginas. I totally get it. I'm not mad.

"It is possible," Dr. Gonzalez says, trying to be gentle. She reminds me of someone approaching a spooked horse. Quiet voice. No sudden movements.

"But we used protection," I tell her. "Every single time."

Dr. Gonzalez has the nerve to just shrug and smile, like my whole world hasn't just been flipped upside down.

"These things do happen sometimes," she says. "There's a small chance of pregnancy, even when you take all of the necessary precautions."

Small chance.

My life has been a series of small chances up to this point.

Small chance of landing an internship at one of the world's most highly sought-after places in New York, Duke Capital.

Small chance of having an unbearably hot CEO run into me—literally—leading to him wearing the coffee I was carrying.

Small chance of his ex-wife hiring me to seduce him so that he would divorce her.

Small chance of the same CEO billionaire being perfect.

Small chance of me falling in love with him.

Small chance of him falling in love with me.

Small chance of him finding out about his ex-wife hiring me.

Small chance of everything falling apart.

Small chance of us coming back together.

And now.

This.

The smallest chance of all, so of course it's happened.

A baby.

My baby. Our baby. Just the thought makes me touch my stomach. Nothing feels different than a few minutes ago, but suddenly, everything feels charged. It's not like my stomach does anything—other than grumble because I'm sort of hungry—but I know that I'm pregnant. And that changes everything.

"And you're sure there's no chance this is a mistake," I try, one more time, because what the fuck. Sure, I should stop swearing now that I'm going to be a mom, but what the actual fuck?

"Well, we can do a pelvic ultrasound to be absolutely sure," Dr. Gonzalez says. "Would you like to do that?"

Honestly, having Dr. Gonzalez examine my pelvis is about the last thing I want, but there's no way in hell that I'm leaving here without being absolutely sure.

"Yes," I agree, likely far too eagerly. "Let's do that."

She gets some gel and squirts it on my stomach. It's warm, which I wasn't expecting, and then she grabs some sort of wand-looking contraption and runs it across my abdomen.

She watches a screen next to her, so I decide to watch that screen, too.

And there, on that screen, is…well, it doesn't really look like anything to me. A bunch of lines, squiggly and strange. But whatever it is, it makes Dr. Gonzalez smile.

"There it is," she says. "There's your baby."

My stomach tightens. The words still don't make sense. How could I possibly be having a baby?

"We can talk about your options," Dr. Gonzalez says.

"Or, if you need some time to process, we can make an appointment for later."

My mind is reeling. What will Harrison say when I tell him?

The reeling hits a hard stop when it slams into reality.

Harrison doesn't want to be a father.

Hasn't he said as much so many times? Like when Ramon's kids were running around like crazy at the party. Or those kids on the ferry. He's made his lack of interest in children pretty clear.

Apparently, he forgot to relay that message to his eager, freakish sperm.

I was hoping that today's visit would lead to a sexy surprise for him, and now? Harrison's in for a whole different surprise.

The kind that I have no idea how to reveal to him.

After I leave the doctor's office—a second appointment booked and a packet of pregnancy information in hand—I attempt to mentally run through the different ways I can break the news to Harrison.

So, Harrison, you know how you hate kids? Good news, I hear they're way less annoying when they're your own!

Ugh, that definitely won't work. And I hate to even think about Harrison not liking his own kid...not that he'll actively dislike the kid, right? Sometimes I like things I didn't think I'd like, like pistachio ice cream, but this is not the same as ice cream so that analogy is crap.

I need a different angle. One that appeals to Harrison's likes.

I could always focus on my original reason for going to the doctor's office.

Guess what, Harrison. Turns out we can have all the sex we want without getting pregnant because I'm already pregnant but hey, no condoms!

Will he even be into me now that I'm knocked up? Sure, I look the same right now, but I won't for long. Will he be completely repulsed by me? I think about the pregnant women I knew back home. Sweating and swollen on the front porch, barking out orders for more decaf sweet tea, complaining about stretch marks.

Oh God.

Home.

Kansas.

I'm going to have to go back.

Harrison's not going to want to have anything to do with me or the baby. And it's not like I can blame him. He said this wasn't what he wanted. So that means I'll have to go it alone, and I can't go it alone in New York. Not even on my new salary.

Which means...

I've only got one option.

Kansas.

Even though I'd decided it wasn't for me.

Even though I'm falling back in love with New York.

Even though I'm already in love with Harrison Duke.

I'm going to start crying in the lobby of the doctor's office if I think about it too much. I can't afford to do that, not when I need to head back to work. I check the time and see that I've already taken the longest of long lunches, even for a client lunch.

I don't even bother to attempt to find my own way back to the office. I've got bigger issues than transportation so I text Bruce for a ride and send him a pin of my location.

Then I pace the sidewalk, as much as one can pace a New York sidewalk without completely annoying everyone trying to power walk from point A to point B. I touch my stomach, still feeling that phantom sensation that something else is part of me now. It doesn't kick or acknowledge me in any way, but it's there.

No, not it. It's a baby.

My baby.

Harrison's baby.

Despite everything, I smile. As terrified as I am, there's something strange and magical about the fact that I'm carrying a baby. Harrison's baby. I'm going to be a mom.

The warm, fuzzy, shocking, overwhelming feeling's still hanging over me when Bruce pulls up. I open the door myself and slide into the back seat before he's even had a chance to put the car in park to do it for me.

"I had an appointment," I babble, like he cares. I'm flustered. I think I'm already sweating. Fantastic.

Bruce just nods. I wonder if, somehow, he knows that I'm pregnant, but that's impossible. I didn't know that I was pregnant an hour ago. No one can tell. No one knows.

But that won't last forever. All too soon it'll be evident to everyone.

I'm still gnawing on the inside of my cheek when I make it to the office. I glance at the Starbucks downstairs and worry about the coffee I had earlier. I'm pretty sure that's not allowed, but I'm not all the way sure. I know sushi's a no-no, but everything else? I'm totally in the dark. Have I already harmed the baby because I needed a latte?

Fuck.

I'm not ready for this at all.

My feet carry me straight to Harrison's office, and I breathe the smallest sigh of relief when I see him inside, alone. His eyes lift to find me as I knock on the open door. He smiles, the best kind of smile, the one he always reserves just for me. I could die right here under that smile.

But first.

Baby.

Baby.

Baby.

Just tell him. The longer I wait the weirder it'll get. He'll be all, why didn't you tell me an hour ago or a week ago or before you gained twenty-five pounds?

I take a breath.

"Harrison—"

"So," he says, twirling a pen around his fingers. "You have something you need to tell me?"

What?

How does he already know?

And what the hell am I going to do now?

CHAPTER TWO

HARRISON

EARLIER I'D STOPPED by Emery's desk to see if she was free for lunch only to hear from her co-workers that she'd dashed off for a client meeting. I thought it was odd because I didn't remember her mentioning it this morning and normally Emery will talk my ear off with all her ideas. But then I remembered the way that Emery's lips had curved into a smile this morning when we went our separate ways to our separate desks.

Like she had a secret.

A naughty secret.

She probably ran out to buy some sexy lingerie or something. Actually, I don't have a clue where the fuck she went, but teasing her is fun.

It said a lot that, even when I didn't know exactly where Emery had snuck off to, I didn't suspect anything shitty. There was a tiny blip of a thought, one brought on from years of my ex-wife Blythe's bullshit, that maybe she was doing something nefarious, but it evaporated quickly.

This was Emery, and if she was doing something on the sly, I knew it would be *for* me. Not to hurt me.

Emery loves me.

She'd proven that in Kansas, and she'd proven it again when she moved back to New York with me.

With Emery, everything is better. I wasn't nearly as much of an asshole with her lighting up the office. I know this, because Sandy told me when she brought me coffee this morning. Even Ramon couldn't stop talking about the way Emery made me less of a dick.

I would've been annoyed, except they were right.

Life was good.

It was why the ring I'd bought for Emery—back before I found that check—sat somewhat heavy in my pocket. I carried it with me almost everywhere and only left it in my nightstand drawer if I worried it might get lost somewhere. I hadn't been able to bring myself to return it after everything seemingly fell apart. But that was clearly because I knew that that ring was meant for Emery's hand, even if we had to sort through some minor bullshit to get there.

Now, I just had to propose. But there wasn't a rush. We were still in the fun phase, the part that was all fun and sex and some more sex on top of that. It was like the honeymoon and we weren't even engaged yet.

And God, just seeing her breeze into my office, all flushed as she closes the door behind her, her teeth sinking into her bottom lip, all I can think is how right this is and how much I want her.

"Go ahead then, tell me," I encourage her, enjoying this little flirtation. You'd think she'd already be immune to blushing around me but she's flustered and now my hopes are high. I wonder if she—

"So condoms," she blurts out, interrupting a delightful fantasy I was conjuring up of Emery blushing her way through a sex-toy store.

I raise a brow in question, hating to end this just yet. I have to admit, I was hoping for something a bit more risqué than flavored condoms assuming that's where this conversation is headed—

"They're so—" she starts again and now I get it and I can't keep the grin off my face.

Fuck yes.

"Inconvenient," I fill in for her.

"Pretty inconvenient," she murmurs while nodding her head. She looks sort of relieved, as if holding this little secret surprise must have been eating her alive.

"I think I know what you're trying to tell me, Emery. And I'm fucking delighted."

"You are?" She looks a bit surprised, her brows rising as we stare at each other. I'm not sure why she's being so shy about this after everything we've done together. But it's cute.

"Of course I am," I tell her, rising from my chair. "Why wouldn't I be? I've been dying to fuck you bare without worrying about the consequences. Thank you for taking care of it."

"Right," she murmurs, staring at my chest as I cross the room to reach her.

I close the last few feet between us and tip her chin up so that her lips meet mine. The kiss turns hungry almost immediately when I think about what we can do now. When I think about how it'll feel to be inside her, nothing between us. Just the thought makes all the remaining blood rush to my cock.

She must feel me harden against her because she lets out a small moan and presses closer against me, moving her hand so that her fingers graze the outline of my cock through my pants.

"So how long do I have to wait?" I ask her. "To fuck you without a condom?"

"Oh." She blinks as if she's forgotten what we were even discussing.

I love that I have this effect on her.

I drop my lips to her jaw, kissing down further to her neck, relishing as she shivers as she considers my words.

"A week maybe?" she finally says, but it's more of a question than an answer.

"Longest week ever," I mutter as I nip at her collarbone, and she lets out a cry of pleasure. I grab her and lift her up so that I'm holding her by her ass, and then I carry her over to the desk so that I can drop her on the edge. She feels so good against me, her breasts fuller than ever, spilling out of her top.

"How do you get hotter every fucking day?" I demand, kissing her again, flicking my tongue into her mouth to taste her.

"I—I could ask the same about you," she says, moaning as I lift a hand to cup her breast through her top. She throws her head back, panting, seemingly already at a fucking ten.

I let one hand drift down until I reach her thighs, and then I slide it up under her skirt. With my thumb, I tease her sweet pussy through her panties.

Fuck. She's soaked all the way through. For me.

"You naughty girl," I say. "A surprise and a pussy that's this wet? I'm going to have to thank you for this."

I drop down to my knees in front of the desk and her spread thighs, pulling her to the edge so that I can kiss along the inside of her legs. She gasps above me, unable to form words as I kiss closer and closer to her swollen lips.

"Take off your top for me," I ask. "I'm dying to see those tits."

She does, dropping her top and bra onto the floor as I continue to kiss her thighs. I add in circles with my tongue, teasing closer and closer to where her pussy waits for me.

Above me, she looks so gloriously full. Her tits bounce as she arches her back, trying to guide me closer and closer to her entrance. But I have to look. And then, I have to touch, reaching up to cup one of them in my hands. Her skin is so incredibly smooth and soft, her nipples hard and peaked under my fingertips. She reacts intensely to each of my touches, bucking her hips and running her tongue over her lips. As if she can't handle it, like she's more sensitive, more hot for me than ever before.

"Please, Harrison," she begs. "Please."

I push her knees back together and pull her panties off slowly, then her skirt. And then there she is, bare for me, pink and swollen and just waiting for my tongue. I part her legs again and then run the tip of my tongue along the inside of her pussy's lips, and she shudders. Finally, I oblige her, letting my tongue drift over and then inside of her.

She grips the desk hard, and I use my hands to reach around and grab her ass, anchoring her to the desk as I plunge in and out of her, savoring the taste of her. She's sweeter today, perfect and delicious as I flatten my tongue against her clit, dying at the sound of those little moans she keeps trying to smother.

Her orgasm shatters through her quickly, each inch of her body flushing pink as she leans back, nearly falling off the desk as the pleasure ripples through her. But I hold her in place, watching her chest as it heaves with each breath that she catches. I stand up and tug her body forward so that I can kiss her and look into her eyes.

Because all of her is perfect, but nothing is quite as good as the way she looks at me after this. After I've given her the kind of pleasure that no one ever has and no one ever will. The moment when she's completely and totally mine.

"Are you ready?" I ask her.

She's still catching her breath, but she nods. I undo my belt and tug down my pants, letting my cock spring forth between us. Pre-cum beads the tip, and it throbs hard in my hand. I slide a condom on, suddenly hating it more than usual now that I know how close we are to not needing them at all. Then I move forward, closer to the edge of the desk, and Emery parts her thighs, her still slick pussy ready and waiting for me.

I slide inside of her in one motion, letting her take me deep inside of her. Emery gasps at the intensity of it, of the feel of us knitted together. The feeling is incredible, like she's swallowing me completely, and every nerve on my cock stands at attention. It's so much that I nearly come right there, but I force myself to go slow, to thrust into her with care. But it's hard to not just come completely undone. In this moment, Emery's more than everything. She's my future, completely and totally.

I move my hands to her back, holding her up as I drive into her, and she wraps her legs around me, letting me in deeper, even though that doesn't seem possible. When the orgasm rips through me, I don't just see stars. I see moons and planets and every other goddamn thing in the universe.

And then, when I open my eyes, I see her.

And it's better than I could've ever dreamed.

After we've cleaned up, she tugs on her panties and then her skirt, a look of flushed pleasure lingering on her cheeks as she does.

"Hope that's enough motivation to help you get through the rest of the day," I say with a grin.

She laughs, but it's soft and quiet.

"I don't know," she says. "I think you might've worn me out."

I can't help it. I stand up a little straighter. I knew it was good, but was it so good that it took it out of her? That's a new record, considering Emery's usually raring to go for one or two more rounds.

"Well," I say, tossing her bra and blouse over to her. "If you need to take the rest of the day, there's no problem with that."

Her eyes widen. "Really?"

"Emery, banging the boss does have some perks. Leave early if you need to."

She smiles, pulling on the rest of her clothes. She checks her lipstick with her phone camera and runs her hand through her hair. Then, she scrolls through, and I see a glimpse of her calendar on the screen.

"I guess I could save these things for tomorrow," she says.

"And it is your fault I'm exhausted."

Damn right it is.

I cross the room and brush my lips against hers.

"Go home," I say. "Rest up. Don't forget about later."

"Right," she says, but her phone's pinged again, and I can tell she's not really listening. Damn. She really is tired.

She gives me one last kiss and then heads for the door. Watching her leave gives me a view of her supple ass, and it takes everything in me not to chase her and fuck her again.

I shouldn't be acting like a horny frat boy. I have work to do. But all I can think about is Emery, perfect Emery with her glorious tits and talented mouth.

Maybe it's time to whisk her off to France. Maybe it's time to put that ring on her finger.

Because now that I have her back, I want it to be permanent. I want her forever.

Just the two of us, with the rest of our lives ahead of us.

CHAPTER THREE

EMERY

I ALMOST FALL asleep in Bruce's car. It's embarrassing when he has to clear his throat when we get back to Harrison's building and my eyes have shut. I mumble an apology to him and stumble out of the car, making excuses about not sleeping well and being overworked then running up to the entrance before he can doubt me.

I wasn't lying to Harrison. He *did* wear me out. But something tells me that I was doomed to be exhausted for the rest of the day even if we didn't have amazing sex at the office.

Is it the pregnancy? Or is it the shock? The fact that I got hit with the news out of nowhere and now I have to figure out what to do with my life?

Whatever it is, it's completely drained me. I head upstairs immediately, and even though I've seen it before, obviously, I'm jarred by the sight of this incredible place that is somehow my home.

It's the kind of place that I thought only existed in the movies. Giant couches, giant TVs, giant windows, giant kitchen...everything ornate and perfect, everything expensive. And it's impeccably kept up during the day with a staff of cleaners and chefs and people to run clothes off to the dry cleaners and people who shop for the clothes in the first place. All I have to do is write a note asking for something, and the next day, it'll appear like magic.

I've never lived like this before. Back on the farm, everything revolved around chores, and it wasn't until the very long list of to-dos was done that I ever got the chance to do anything. Even the first time around in New York, I spent my weekends hustling to the laundromat or at the grocery store. Now, living with Harrison, my days are for work and then, when that's done, for myself. And for Harrison. It's still odd to me, and sometimes I have to insist on doing some things on my own. Like making the bed or washing dishes. It just seems ridiculous that anyone else would do those things for me.

A two-floor apartment, in Manhattan. We have a gym and a small library, inside the apartment. It's all like something out of a dream, and I'm still pinching myself that, somehow, I get to live here. For now.

Right now, though, I'm not interested in the gym or the library or even the kitchen. There is one thing on my mind, and that's the enormous bed, its million thread count, and its fluffy comforter and blankets. I don't even change my clothes. I just plop down on top of it all, grab one of the many pillows, and shut my eyes. Almost immediately, I fall asleep. Exhaustion, apparently, is nature's melatonin.

I'm out for hours. I can tell when I wake up that it's been way, way, way too long for a nap. I'm pretty sure I was dreaming, a deep dream that made me question, just for a moment, if today actually happened.

But of course it did.

The notifications from my phone don't lie. There's an email from my doctor's office letting me know that I can review my medical records online if I want to. Lucky me. There's also a reminder from Dr. Gonzalez about my next appointment. I wish I could ignore it for a little while longer, but there's no way. Something tells me that this pregnancy is going to fly by faster than I expect. Especially since I missed the first month or so by not even knowing.

Then there's the fact that I still need to tell Harrison what's going on. Because that definitely can't wait nine months. On the way home with Bruce, I'd had a vague idea about napping, then pulling myself together to do a quiet dinner at home where I could break the news to him. I guess I can still do that second part. I'll just go take a quick shower to help myself wake up.

I start to sit up and rub my eyes open. Then, from behind me, I hear the tell-tale sign of Harrison and his footsteps.

"There's my sleeping beauty," he says with a smile. "Someone really was tired."

I fight a yawn and fail.

"Well, hopefully the rest helped prepare you for tonight," Harrison says.

I blink. Tonight? What's he talking about?

He clearly reads my expression. "Don't you remember? I reminded you about it back at the office, right before you left. We have dinner at Ramon's."

Oh God.

All of a sudden, I remember that yes, earlier this week, we promised to do dinner with Ramon and his family. It sounded like a great way to bond with another couple. But now, we're bonding with another *family*. Not that Harrison has any idea about that last part.

"Shit," I say. "I forgot."

"Don't worry," Harrison says. "Why don't you just get ready, and I'll text Ramon and let him know we're running a little late."

He kisses me, and memories of earlier flood back to me. Sex, his office. Harrison thinking we're counting down the days until we can fuck without a condom, not counting down the months until we're covered in burp clothes and baby vomit.

But I don't have time to think about that now, not with Harrison and dinner waiting. I hop up out of bed and head to the bathroom to check the damage that the nap wrecked on me. My outfit from today's completely wrinkled and too "office" anyway, so I change into a flowy maxi skirt and loose top. My hair's now standing firmly frizzed to one side, so I comb it out and twist it up into a casual updo. Brush my teeth, dab at where my mascara ran a little during the day, and then I add a new swipe of lipstick. There. Perfectly presentable.

And pregnant.

Not that anyone else knows that last part.

I head out to the living area and give Harrison a twirl of my skirt. He laughs.

"You're radiant today," he muses, staring at me for a long moment.

I blush. Oh no. He's definitely going to figure this out.

I'm not going to be able to keep this under wraps much longer.

"I think the nap worked some miracles," I deflect in response.

"It was before the nap," Harrison argues, leading us towards the door.

He's so on to me.

"What can I say? New York agrees with me." I shrug, hoping he'll drop it because we absolutely cannot have this conversation right now.

"Yeah, well, hopefully you can keep that attitude after Ramon's demon spawn wreak havoc tonight."

I almost bite my tongue off trying not to react to those words. God, he really does hate kids. There's no way he'll be happy about having his own. But I manage to put on a happy face as he links his arm in mine and guides us out into the hall, down the elevator, and into the car.

I can just ignore being pregnant for a little longer. Right? Just for tonight? Maybe I'll make a nice breakfast tomorrow or something.

I'll figure it out.

Ramon and his family live in a brownstone in Brooklyn. There's no front yard, but it's positively suburban in comparison to Harrison's high-rise. As Bruce pulls to the curb, I admire the block, an entire row of brownstones complete with a few kids playing in the front on scooters. There's a couple walking with a giant stroller. There's a stray frisbee on the steps outside of Ramon's house. It's all so homey. Nothing like the impeccable kid-free environment Harrison keeps.

Ramon opens the door grinning and wearing an apron that says, "Kiss the Cook!" He waves us in, and the house is cute, full of cozy touches and framed photos of their family. He walks us over to the family room where there's a leather chair that's clearly been loved for years, along with a dark gray couch that's currently got

Ramon's wife lounging on it, her feet up as she reads a magazine.

"There you two are!" Anita says, sitting up from the couch. I'd forgotten that she's pregnant, too, and she's definitely swollen in size since the last time I saw her. Or maybe I'm just imagining things. Still, she manages to look effortlessly pretty, with her hair swept back behind a pearl-colored headband.

"Apologies. It takes me a second to get off the couch these days," Anita says, rubbing her protruding stomach. "But I'll be right there."

"Take your time," Harrison says.

"Yes, don't stress yourself out, *mi amor*," Ramon says, eyes twinkling in her direction. "I'm still working on dinner."

"Nonsense," Anita says, sauntering over to us. I have to force myself not to look at her pregnant belly. She makes it look easy, but I know that it isn't. And I also know that I've got nine months of this ahead of me. Or eight. Or something. I will myself not to panic.

She pulls me into a hug. "So good to see you."

It really is good to see her. There's something about Ramon's family that just exudes warmth. But I feel guilty hugging her, like somehow she'll sus me out and know that I'm pregnant too just by touching me.

She looks over her shoulder and calls to one of the rooms I can't see.

"Gabriela, Cesar, come out here. Emery and Harrison are here for dinner."

Immediately, I hear the rush of little feet running around the corner. Gabriela appears in the hallway, looking ridiculously cute in a little green dress. She breaks into a smile and rushes over to me, throwing her little arms around my legs.

"Emery," she says.

"She's been so excited that you were coming," Ramon explains. "She hasn't stopped talking about you since the party."

My heart has officially melted when Gabriela turns her shining eyes up at me. She turns to Harrison, and I check to see if he, also, is having his heart melted. But his expression is neutral.

"Where's the other one?" Harrison asks.

Ramon laughs. "You mean my son?"

"Yes," Harrison says. "I just—"

"POW!"

Ramon's son, a tiny version of himself, appears behind Harrison, poking him in the back with some kind of Nerf gun. I have to stifle a laugh.

"Cesar," Anita says, crossing her arms. "What did I tell you? No Nerf guns in the house."

"POW!" Cesar says again, streaking away before either of his parents can grab him.

Ramon sighs. "Sorry about that. Apparently, three hours at the park didn't quite tire him out yet."

"Should I be on the lookout for more attacks?" Harrison asks, attempting a shrug as if he's totally comfortable being attacked by a Nerf-wielding child.

He's not.

I remind myself that he's probably never been around kids. He's an only child. It's not like he grew up babysitting as a side hustle. Right?

He'll adapt. With some practice.

Maybe.

Ramon smirks. "Possibly. But come have a seat in the living room. I'll bring snacks."

We work our way through spinach artichoke dip and chips, something far less extravagant than anything I can imagine Harrison eating. And truthfully, he seems a little out of place here, in this family home. And maybe I'm the one eating all the dip. But he seems to be enjoying himself, in a polite way. While on the lookout for foam bullets and sticky fingers.

Meanwhile I keep looking at Anita's belly, so much so that, at some point, she smiles at me and tells me her due date.

"It's not quite as awful as it looks," she offers up, in a reassuring tone.

I freeze, deer in headlights, hoping Harrison didn't overhear.

"Oh no," I say quickly. "You just look really beautiful. That pregnancy glow, you know."

I force a laugh, but it sounds too high.

"Ha!" Anita says. "That glow's from sweating all day as I chase these two rascals around. But thank you. I appreciate it anyway."

I nod. I manage to avoid any pregnancy talk for the rest of appetizers, and everything feels safe until dinner. That is, until Cesar materializes with a juice box that he promptly spills on Harrison's suit.

I bite my lip, already on the edge with nerves, waiting for Harrison to explode on the kid. But he just laughs and turns to me.

"This kid is your protégé," he says, still laughing. "God, just imagine the nightmare of a mini-you, spilling on me all the time."

I laugh, swallowing some of my water too hard so that I almost choke. Harrison pats my back, giving me a weird look, but thankfully, Gabriela saves me by insisting on telling me about her collection of Disney princesses. I've never looked more interested in anything in my entire life.

"We need a vacation," Harrison says to me after Gabriela takes a pause to ingest some macaroni and cheese. "I've been thinking about that ever since we got back."

I don't answer. I just focus on my food and nod, hoping the crazy smile that I've fixed on my face hasn't fallen off.

Harrison turns to Ramon. "I was thinking about booking a wine tour in the South of France in a few months. When business gets a little slower."

A wine tour? In France? Any other time, I'd be jumping at the chance to travel to France. I've wanted to go there my entire life, ever since I read *Madeline* when I was a kid. I wanted to wear a little yellow hat and go to the Eiffel Tower and take pictures. Now, I'm an adult, and the idea is still just as magical—just with alcohol.

Alcohol I can't even have. I had to dodge the question tonight, lying and saying my stomach felt off and that maybe my lunch was bad or something. Well, it was only partly a lie. My stomach does feel off, which has to be nerves. There's no way I found out I was pregnant and then immediately started having symptoms. That would be the worst luck ever.

Then again, my luck's been a little off today.

But a wine tour in France? I definitely won't be able to go. I'll be a house, too huge for the plane seats, even the nice cushy ones on Harrison's private plane. And even if I do fit, I'm definitely going to be hideous. I won't be able to pull it off like Anita. I've seen pictures of my mother pregnant. Cankles. I'm going to have cankles.

"I'm so jealous," Ramon says. "We won't be able to plan a trip like that for another decade."

"A decade?" Harrison looks doubtful. "Try two decades, more like. You're starting all over again with the third."

"You mean you don't want to babysit for us?" Anita teases, waving her fork in Harrison's direction. "While we jet off to France?"

They all laugh, but I can't even come up with a fake one. Because I've realized that, at some point, I won't even be *able* to fly. And even if we go before I hit that magical barrier, I'll still be the pregnant and sober ball and chain, waddling along behind Harrison, sniffing his discarded wineglasses for a hint of what I'm missing.

The talk turns to refills, with Harrison and Ramon leaving the table together to fill glasses. Cesar bounces after them while Gabriela continues to inhale her macaroni.

"So, do you think you're going to have children?" Anita asks, blinking at me politely.

Do I think? No, Anita, I *know*. But I also know that there's no way Harrison will want any part of a life like this, not with its chaos and its macaroni.

"We have not had the conversation," I tell her through gritted teeth.

CHAPTER FOUR

HARRISON

I DON'T UNDERSTAND why Emery's been so squirrely. Last night, when Ramon and I came back to the dinner table, she was quiet and looked like she was almost in pain. But then she caught my eyes and smiled like nothing was wrong.

Still, there's no escaping the fact that, once we were home again, she took a long shower and was asleep in bed before we could even talk, let alone fuck like I'd hoped. Then, this morning, she gotten ready quietly, and something was clearly on her mind. I tried to ask, but she just smiled and said she was just thinking ahead about something she needed to do at work.

It's not that I don't believe her. I'm sure she's still getting used to everything, so that might be part of it, but it certainly isn't the whole story. There's something else, something off, but I just don't know what.

"Well, you sort of just dove back into reality, didn't you?" Ramon says, considering the question I just posed about Emery.

I don't love asking him for help, but I don't know who else I would ask. And it sort of just bubbled up out of me when we went to lunch to talk strategy about some of the newer accounts. Besides, Ramon's a man I trust. And he's the only one that I know that knows anything at all about women.

"I mean, what else were we supposed to do?" I ask. "She came back, she got the job, she started working. I would've loved for her to take a break, but that's not what she wanted."

"Hmm," Ramon says, sipping his coffee. "Well, maybe it's one thing to want something and another to get it."

"This was sudden," I say. "She's been fine ever since we got back. No, not fine. Overjoyed. You've seen her. This has been just over the last few days."

"Did something happen? Blythe, maybe?"

I consider that. There's nothing concrete I can point to, other than the trip to the doctor. But she was thrilled about that outcome. And work's been fine. Blythe's been suspiciously quiet, yes, but quiet nonetheless.

"Honestly, I don't have any idea what's going on," I say. "As far as I knew, we were still in that honeymoon phase of dating."

Ramon takes a bite of his sandwich and thinks.

"Maybe everything's just catching up to her," he says. "Or maybe she's questioning whether everything's happening too fast."

"I don't follow," I say. The restaurant we're at is full of white splash walls and greenery crawling up the sides. We're at a table near the back, fairly secluded, but I still feel exposed just talking about this.

"I just mean that you were sort of in this fantasy world

before," he says. "Everything shiny and new. The honeymoon phase, like you said. And then you came back and, suddenly, you were living together. It introduces its own challenges."

"We're still in the honeymoon phase," I say, unable to stop how defensive I sound.

"I know you are," Ramon says. "But now, you're also roommates. Roommates with routines. It takes some of the spontaneity out of it."

I nod. This makes sense. I don't like it, but it does make sense. Maybe Emery's missing some of what we had in Kansas, days where she didn't know what would happen. And we did talk about romance and travel... Clearly, that's what she's craving.

"I can't take another vacation for a few months," I say. "That week in Kansas put me behind."

Ramon laughs. "You don't need a vacation. That's part of being in a good relationship. You have to find ways to make the day-to-day special."

"Like how?"

Ramon smiles. "Whatever she likes, boss. If it's coffee and a breakfast burrito from a place over in Brooklyn, you go there at five in the morning to make sure she has it. If she has a favorite type of pajamas, you buy her ten pairs. It could be as simple as a movie night at home or something bigger. You know this stuff, man. You're going to be fine."

I nod, bringing my own coffee to my lips. He's right. Of course I can do this. I can find a way to impress Emery right here in New York. Hell, this place is a romantic destination all on its own. Countless movies have made this a city to remember. I could look on Emery's list and find something we didn't get to do yet. Something that mixes her love of New York with one of her Kansas girl passions.

It doesn't take long for me to think of it. And when I land on it, I just know that I've got gold.

"I've got it," I tell Ramon.

———

"A SURPRISE?"

I find Emery at her desk at the end of the day and tell her I've got a surprise waiting for us. For some reason, she doesn't look thrilled. In fact, she looks momentarily terrified.

Oh no. Has she already fallen into the routine so much that she is going to resist the surprise?

I push the thought away. Emery's going to love this. I've found a way to combine her love of New York and her love of horses into one activity, and there's no way she won't love it.

"Do I need to go home and change?"

I shake my head. "Nope. What you're wearing now is perfect."

She's in a long dress that hits just past her knees. It's a stretchy material, deep navy blue, and her ass looks incredible in it. Plus, if the surprise goes well, it'll be easy to pull her onto my lap in the limo…

Not that that's what today's about. Today's about Emery and spontaneity and romance. Could those things lead to sex? Sure. But that'll be a bonus.

We head down and get in the car. She and Leo exchange pleasantries, and then we're off. Leo drives us to Central Park. Emery's still oddly quiet, but I know that, soon, she'll be over the moon with excitement for what I've planned.

Thankfully, it seems like I hit the nail on the head, because as soon as Leo gets close enough, a huge smile appears on Emery's face and she plasters herself to the window. Just like she did when we first explored the city together.

"Oooh, Central Park!" Emery coos, staring out at the famous locale.

"It was on your list," I remind her.

She leans back and kisses me, deeply.

"You remembered," she says.

I knew it. I knew I'd chosen the perfect farmgirl activity.

"Come on," I tell her, opening the door and taking her hand.

She squeezes, her eyes wide as she takes in the beauty of Central Park. We do a loop around as she insists on taking pictures, some of her usual glee back in her face. I can't help but feel a wave of pride knowing that I did it, and we haven't even gotten to the best part yet.

We head further into the park, and Emery stops to pet a few dogs. Then, we reach the other side, and I grin at her.

"Ready for the real surprise?"

Her eyes widen. "There's more?"

"It's right over there," I say, and I gesture to where the horse and carriage wait for us.

It's one of the newer carriages with giant wheels and a generous seat, painted white with roses splashed across the front. The horse is a beautiful chestnut color with a black mane that's been braided. It gives us a friendly whinny as we approach.

It's the kind of tourist trap that I usually wouldn't be caught dead in, but for Emery, I don't give a damn. I know she'll be thrilled. I look from the carriage to her, waiting to see her fall to pieces with enthusiasm, but instead, she just sort of…stares at it.

What the hell?

"This is the only way to do Central Park," I tell her. "At least, if you want to do it the way your guidebooks tell you to."

She offers a weak smile. "Then we better get it over with!"

I turn to her. "What?"

"I meant get started," she says quickly. Before I can say anything else, she's launched herself into the carriage.

Confused, I settle in beside her. Emery's supposed to love this crap, but instead, she's strangely silent, even as the horse picks up and clops forward. I tell her what I know, the horse's name, the history of the carriages, shit I learned looking it up earlier, but she's barely listening to me.

In fact, she looks completely miserable.

"Emery?"

She looks quickly at me. "How long does this last?"

Well, fuck, that stings. "Jesus Christ, I thought you'd like this."

"I—"

But she doesn't finish the sentence.

Instead, she projectile vomits all over my shoes.

CHAPTER FIVE

EMERY

OH GOD.

Oh God.

Oh God.

I've never been so embarrassed in my entire life.

Or, okay, that might be an exaggeration. I can think of a few recent examples that were worse.

But this is pretty bad.

Because it was one thing to spill coffee on Harrison Duke when he was my billionaire boss.

It's another thing to throw up on him when he's my boyfriend.

It's totally made worse, too, by the fact that I pretty much flew out of the carriage while the driver started screaming and cursing when he realized what had happened, and then, just to add to my humiliation, I looked back and saw that the only reason he stopped was because Harrison was offering him a giant wad of cash in addition to his apology.

This is exactly why he's going to break it off. There's no

vacationing in France with a pregnant woman. She'll just vomit on your shoes, shoes that you already had to replace at some point because she spilled coffee on them before she was even pregnant.

I feel sick, not just because the carriage felt like a damn roller coaster, but because this is clear evidence that there's no way in hell that Harrison is going to stick with me. This is the end, clear as day, and there's nothing that can be painted over this to make it any better. He's going to offer *me* a wad of cash to raise this baby alone; I can already picture it.

Fuck, I feel like I could vomit again right now.

I need to get back to the center of the park. The air's fresh there, and I think I saw a cart selling bottles of water. I stumble forward, ignoring Harrison calling my name behind me. I have to ignore him because the manure from the horses and the smell of my own lunch's return is making my stomach lurch, and I refuse to do that. Again.

"Emery!"

I turn and see he's chasing after me, looking totally and completely bewildered. He's taken off his shoes—did he have to trash them?—and is holding out his hands in a clear non-verbal expression of "What the hell just happened?"

"I need water," I tell him. "I'm looking for that cart we passed earlier."

"You're going the wrong way," he says. "Just sit tight on that bench, and I'll go get it. Are you okay? Do you need a doctor or something?"

"No," I say quickly. I don't need to be at a doctor's office right now. Just the thought of smelling anything astringent right now…

I cover my mouth.

"I just need water," I force out. "Please."

"Sit down," he says, pointing to the bench behind me. "I'll be right back, okay?"

I nod. It's really all that I have the energy to do. He turns and heads in the other direction, and I bury my face in my hands.

I guess the cat will be out of the bag after this. Harrison's smart. He'll put this together, won't he? No girl just vomits out of nowhere, not unless she's pregnant. Or maybe if she has food poisoning. But something tells me that Harrison's going to figure it out: the doctor visit, my exhaustion, my throwing up just now.

I'd just wanted to tell him more elegantly. I've seen how it's supposed to go on Instagram: big fancy dinner, a wrapped pregnancy test, a tearful hug. But that's when the couple's been trying for a pregnancy. That's when they both want a baby.

But that's not Harrison. Harrison wanted a girlfriend who would travel the world with him. I know he cares about me. I know he loves me. But there are some things that are just too much to get past. It would be easier if we'd had the conversation about no kids, if we were on the same page. But I thought I had time to bring him around to the idea. Maybe spend more time with little Gabriela and less with Cesar. Or maybe he'd warm up to it after we got all of the other stuff out of our systems. When he was ready. When we both were ready.

Tears threaten to spill over, but I refuse to cry in the middle of Central Park. It's just too damn depressing.

Still, tears or no tears, my head's swimming with everything. What am I going to do? I looked up apartments at work today, and even though I could definitely afford one on my new salary, it's not going to come anywhere close to what I'll need for childcare. And even though I know Harrison will take care of us…the idea of being in this city, alone again, is just terrifying. I'll need my mom. It's Kansas or bust.

I almost call her right then. My fingers actually hover over her number, and I try to imagine her reaction. Mom had me and my brother when she was in her early twenties, but that was also just what happened back then. That was Mom's dream. She'd just sent me off with the hope that I would really make something of myself, for me and for her. And as much as being a mom is part of my dream, it's not my only dream.

Harrison. New York. All of this was my dream.

And now…now I'm going to have to adjust.

Harrison shows up several minutes later with two bottles of Voss wearing a pair of fresh new shoes. I blink at them and look at him.

"I called Leo," he says. "They only had Dasani at the stand, and I figured that wouldn't help your, uh, situation. Besides, we always keep a few of these in the car, and it gave me a chance to grab my spare running shoes."

I force a smile as I gulp down the water. He settles down next to me and puts a hand on my back, rubbing it in small circles. I close my eyes, trying to focus on the sensation so that I keep the water down.

"Anyway, once you've gotten your energy back, I've had Leo park closer to us here. We'll get you home, and I can run you a bath. And I was thinking maybe soup, if you're up to it. And then—"

"I just want to go home," I say, not having the energy

to sound nicer about it. He raises an eyebrow but doesn't argue. Instead, he gives me his elbow and helps me up, and I hate it. Hate how vulnerable I feel. Hate how I ruined today.

Because it would've been so sweet, wouldn't it? A carriage ride with the love of my life in Central Park on a beautiful day. I bet he had a nice dinner planned for later, too. But now…now everything has to change.

He must know. That's why he's talking about the bath. The soup. He's being nice, but once I'm feeling better, it'll be a matter of time before he asks me to pack my things.

"Leo's waiting for us," he tells me, and I lean against him as we walk. I feel shaky on my legs, which is ridiculous. I'm not that weak. But leaning lets me close my eyes so that the world doesn't spin, and I can keep from throwing up again.

I don't even acknowledge Leo when we get to the car. I'm feeling more and more like shit, and it takes everything to just sit straight. I have to close my eyes again as the car moves, not able to enjoy my usual window-shopping of the New York streets.

Yet another thing this situation has robbed from me.

Once we're back in the apartment—one slightly precarious elevator ride later—I feel like I can finally breathe again. Harrison goes to run the bath, and I feel like I could cry. This is it. The last niceties I'll get from the best man I've ever known.

"Don't worry," I crack out over the sound of the running water. "I'll be fine. I'll go back to Kansas and my mom will take care of me."

Harrison stops the water and returns to the bedroom, looking at me like I've grown an extra head.

"Why in the world would you go back to Kansas?"

I refuse to cry. I refuse—oh, hell, here they come. The tears. I lift my chin and pray they'll stay put in my tear ducts.

"The public school system is much better than you'd think in Kansas," I tell him.

Harrison snorts. "In *your* hometown? It's probably a one-room schoolhouse! But why do I care about school systems? Is this the fever talking? You probably got the flu from one of Ramon's walking petri dishes."

A fever? *The flu*? Does he really think I'm just sick with the flu? Has he really not put it together that I'm pregnant?

I was wrong.

Apparently, you can be the intelligent, even genius-level CEO of a company and still be obtuse to the facts right in front of you. I'd thought that the cat was out of the bag, but for Harrison, it apparently never even meowed.

"I didn't catch anything from Ramon's kids," I tell him, the tears evaporating at this new development. "I caught it from *you*."

Harrison gawks at me. "Me? But I don't have the flu!"

I roll my eyes. "Neither do I! I'm pregnant."

I cross my arms over my chest and immediately wince. When did my boobs get so damn sore?

And what does Harrison make of this bomb that I've just dropped?

Because so far, he's just staring at me, like somehow, if he stays very, very still, the news won't be real. It takes a moment for him to recover the ability to speak, and when he does, his voice sounds dry.

"How did that happen?"

I glare at him. "At least my one-room schoolhouse taught me science, unlike Billionaire School!"

He holds up his hands, still clearly thunderstruck. "Oh fuck. Okay."

I turn away from him. "It's fine. Like I said. I can go back home."

This will be easier for him. He'll get to keep his life. And me...at least I'll have my memories, right?

But then I feel his hands on my waist, spinning me back to face him.

And oh hell.

There are those eyes, staring down into mine, dark and serious and wanting.

And that expression is back, the one that declares to everyone in the room that he's the boss, and he'll get exactly what he wants.

"What the hell are you talking about?" Harrison says, his voice low and gruff and so fucking delicious.

"I—"

"You think I'd just let you leave? Again? Not. An. Option. Your home is with me."

His lips touch my forehead as he pulls me into his arms. And even if my body feels like it's on the brink of breaking, one kiss from Harrison and it's racing back together.

It might not be a fever, but I'm burning all over.

Because he wants me.

He wants *us*.

And maybe I won't have to leave after all.

CHAPTER SIX

HARRISON

SHE'S PREGNANT.

It doesn't make any sense.

We were so careful.

Once I've got Emery tucked into a bath with a cup of decaffeinated tea and one of her favorite books, I head downstairs to the gym. The soup won't be here for an hour or so, and either way, she says her stomach can't handle it at the moment, anyway.

Because she's pregnant.

With my fucking child.

Somehow.

The first thing I do is hop on the treadmill, starting with a brisk walk for a warm-up. When in doubt about a business decision and the right move, a good run can always lead to a eureka moment, and I've never been in more need of that than right fucking now.

What to do?

It's not that I'm opposed to having a baby. And the fact that Emery's carrying my baby, well, there's nothing more perfect. It's just the timing. And the fact that I thought we had a few more years before this point. Sure, I assumed kids were going to be a part of the picture, but I thought they'd come after a wedding and some world travel and a million more rounds of desk sex.

I turn the treadmill up so that I'm jogging, then sprinting, forward.

I hadn't even gotten to propose yet. The ring's still in my nightstand drawer, waiting. Only I guess there won't be any more waiting. That will have to be the first step. I'll ask for her hand, she'll accept, we'll get married, and I suppose we can just cram the world travel into the next few months.

But then I remember Emery throwing up in the carriage, and even that is clearly going to need to change.

I run for the next twenty minutes until my shirt's sticking to me and sweat's dripping down my temples. I head to the weight rack and grab some dumbbells, numbly pumping through curls as I think everything through.

I had a ten-year plan, but now, everything will have to change. We'll have to get the entire place baby-proofed, get a nursery together, a million things to get done to make sure everything's easy for Emery. We'll have to find a nanny. And one of those doulas for the pregnancy. I don't know what a doula does, exactly, but Ramon's mentioned that Anita has one, and if she does, then clearly Emery will need one, too.

I'll just have to make new plans. I've done it before. Fuck, I had to change my entire life when Blythe decided to detonate our marriage. And that, clearly, was for the best. This will be, too, as long as I can put everything into place.

More curls. Then overhead presses. I work my way around the gym, using each station to think through something else.

But the proposal sticks in my mind as the undeniable first step. I'll just have to ask her. There's no time to do anything else. And besides, she's clearly stressed that we're not married. I still can't believe she was talking about going back to Kansas. How could she even imagine I would allow it?

She must just be missing her mom, I think. It must have been her first thought. But I'll work through arrangements for that, too, at some point.

Still. She was ready to move. I clearly haven't been clear on my commitment. But that will change.

Then there's my own family. Steps to take there, too. I feel like I see a spreadsheet in my future, something to give me a sense of an anchor. There will be calls to make, too. I'll need to put Sandy on a few things.

I head over to the bench and sit down, counting down for a hundred different crunches. Each one reminds me of something else I'll need, and these are just the things I'm aware of. I'm slightly terrified to check online to see what I'm missing because I have no doubt that it's a lot.

Once I've worn my body to exhaustion, it's time for a shower. I use the one downstairs in the gym, letting the water wash away all of the sweat and grime. Being in the shower reminds me of Emery, of the feel of her naked body against mine, the water slicking our skin. The way her hair looks when it's wet and the feel of her hand around my cock. I wish I could pull her down here right now and devour her with my mouth, but then I remember she's in the bath, body numb and exhausted from today's activities. But I've got a clearer head than I've had in a few hours.

I have a new plan, at least. And that's a start.

When I get back upstairs to our bedroom, Emery's already tucked under the sheets. The soup's been stowed in the fridge. I could wake her up, but she probably needs sleep more than anything so I head to the living room for a glass of whiskey.

We can do this, I tell myself, trying not to think about Ramon's son and his affinity for weapons. That's a clear example of just needing stricter boundaries, which I can provide. Ramon's an excellent worker and father, but he's more lax than I am. I'll be able to pull it together. Clear guidelines, that's the ticket to easy parenthood.

Besides, our kid will be amazing, right? A little version of her, hopefully, rather than a grump like me. I smile at the thought. I hope they get her eyes, her hair, her everything, honestly.

But if they do, that will make them all the harder to discipline. Is that why Ramon has such a hard time of it? Does he look at little Cesar and see Anita?

Or is it one of those instances where I can't even know what I don't know? I'm sure that's what Ramon would tell me. He'd say that I might know how to run a company but being a parent is a whole different ballgame.

Then how the hell is anyone supposed to prepare? I pull out my phone and look up fifty different pregnancy and parenting manuals, but they all seem to contradict each other. I have nowhere to even begin.

Before I know it, I'm pacing.

Something tells me I've got a lot of that in my future.

CHAPTER SEVEN

EMERY

HARRISON'S DOING a terrible job of hiding his mental breakdown.

He thinks he's being super slick, heading down to the gym to work out, as if I don't know that's where he goes when he's beyond stressed and trying to work out the problem.

And right now?

Right now, I'm the problem.

The super fertile, super pregnant problem.

The girl who apparently demolishes perfectly good condoms with her uterus so that she can get knocked up.

I know that he said he wanted me here, but isn't it possible that he secretly hates me for this? Is he just trying to do the right thing even though he's going to be miserable?

Because the last thing I want is for him to be miserable.

In fact, Harrison's happiness is pretty much more important to me than anything else. His smile is a drug, and I've been hooked on it, willing to do anything and everything to put that little grin on his face.

But now? Now, I'm the cause of him doing a thousand bench presses so that he can work off the furious steam from finding out that I'm pregnant.

There go all of his plans, obviously. Anything fun that he wanted to do is just up in smoke.

I might be able to tell myself that I'm being silly, that he's clearly just exercising, if he didn't come back and proceed to pace around the room with a glass of whiskey, ice tinkling in his glass and he does laps around and around. He thinks I've fallen asleep, obviously, but how could I possibly sleep right now? Especially as I hear him mumbling, catching words like "first step" and "rethink that."

He's clearly upset. Hell, animals home on the farm are more discreet.

God, what if he thinks I'm like Blythe and that I've done this so that I hitched my wagon to his forever just for his money? If he doesn't already, the resentment will grow and fester forever, and someday, we'll be fighting about how I took this as a golden ticket to suck the money out of him forever.

I'm close to hyperventilating, but then I have to stop.

Because it doesn't really matter what Harrison does right now. I have a baby to worry about, but more immediately, I have myself to worry about. If there's now a ticking clock on what I can make happen, then I need to do everything I can in the next few months to put my life on the right track. After all, I've got months to go before I'll even be thinking about being barefoot and pregnant in the kitchen.

It's just up to me to make them count, and that starts with getting enough sleep. I turn away from the open bedroom door, snuggle into the covers, and breathe in the scent of Harrison's shampoo that clings to them.

Let Harrison stress out there in the living room.

I've got to focus on me.

———

IN THE MORNING, I shower and decide that this is all mind over matter. I'm barely pregnant, right? This has got to be the time when it's easy. All of that vomiting and feeling sore and achy was in my head because this is just the beginning and, like everything in life, it must get worse over time. I don't look pregnant, anyway, so why would I feel pregnant?

I think maybe I'll call my doctor today and get her tips on making this as smooth as possible. Maybe she'll give me some magic herbs that I can eat to make this as easy as pie. I bet my mom will have some tips, too, though I'm not totally sure I'm ready for that conversation. At least not yet.

After the shower, I brush my teeth. Harrison's headed down to the gym again, which is a blessing in disguise because this toothpaste tastes different today and...

Well, good thing I haven't had breakfast yet.

I brush again, fighting off a second wave as I remind myself that this is all in my head. I'm just feeling this way because of nerves. Then, I pick out one of my favorite new power outfits to pull on. It's a peach-colored suit jacket, loose white top, and matching peach skirt with kitten heels, and it all still looks perfect on me. Which, of course it does. Because I'm barely pregnant and have no reason to stress.

I'm swiping on lipstick when Harrison appears, freshly showered from downstairs. I watch him in the mirror as he pulls on his suit, looking devilishly good. He catches me looking and smiles.

"Don't start looking at me like that," he says with a smirk. "Or we'll be late to the office."

Which, today, we can't afford. Harrison woke up to a call from Sandy asking if he could be in a virtual meeting with Germany first thing this morning. Something to do with one of their major accounts expanding. Plus, I have my own meeting with Monica from Pink to go over some new feature that they're adding to the platform that they want to highlight in upcoming marketing material.

"Right," I say. "I'll just go get our stuff together."

The chef has been leaving packed lunches lately, and I find that mine's a delicious-looking chicken salad, some fruit, and almonds. I realize that, now, I'm eating for two. Is all of this pregnancy friendly? I'll have to do some googling when I get to work.

I also need to see if there's something to make me feel less nauseous. I remember Mom used to always give us ginger tea when we had stomachaches, so I rifle through the cabinets on the hunt for some—to no avail. Harrison's not really a tea drinker in general and only has some decaf green tea. I leave a note for the staff asking if they can grab some ginger tea for the future.

Harrison comes out with three different tie options, looking somewhat grumpy.

"Which one says 'please stop fucking up things that should be easy' to my employees?" Harrison asks.

I smile. Well, at least he's getting back to normal. Maybe the working out/pacing last night got all his worries out. Or, at least, some of them.

"The red one," I say. "Color of confidence."

"And blood," Harrison points out. "Which works."

After he's put on the tie, we head to the office. Harrison ends up taking the call from Germany in the car, where he does a lot of berating that gets translated to the German office. Lots of strong consonants, which doesn't sound great. But when we get there, he smiles at me.

"I'll grab us coffee," he says.

I bite my lip, glancing at Leo as we shut the car door behind us. Once he drives away, I say, "Pretty sure I have to be off coffee for a bit."

Harrison looks almost as shocked as when I said I was pregnant.

"Really?"

"I haven't done a ton of research, to be honest," I admit. "But I'm going to call my doctor today."

"When are you going back?" Harrison asks. "I have some questions of my own."

I laugh. "Oh, you do?"

He nods, not elaborating. He probably wants to ask her if I'm really, truly pregnant.

"It's next week," I say. "I'll text you the details."

He grins. "Emery, we live and work together. I'm pretty sure the text isn't necessary."

It feels almost normal, except for that we're talking about the fact that I'm carrying his child. My hand absently goes to my stomach, and Harrison's eyes follow it.

"Can you feel anything yet?"

I shake my head. "No. But I keep checking. You know, just in case."

He presses a kiss to my forehead.

"We're in this together, Kansas," he says. "And you're staying put."

It's so sweet, and I want to believe it. I want to believe that he's really on board, but it's hard to do when I remember how he's acted around any kid ever. And then my stomach does a flip that I don't think is totally related to the forehead kiss, and I know that I need to get somewhere with a trash can or a toilet and fast.

"I don't want you to be late for your next meeting," I tell him.

"And I don't want you to be late for yours," he replies.

Once we get to the office, I make a beeline for the porcelain chamber, empty my stomach, and then get to work. My email box is semi-slammed, but I clear fifty or so emails easily. I'd love to get to inbox zero before moving onto anything else, but my stomach's still turning. I decide to take a quick field trip over to Sandy's desk to ask her if we have any ginger tea, and she gives me a look when I do.

"Food poisoning," I say, knowing that I've probably immediately turned beet red. I hate lying to Sandy. She's been sweet to me ever since the beginning, and even if we're not ready to tell people, I still feel like shit.

"I'll get you some," she says.

"Oh, I can—"

"Don't you worry," she says with a conspiratorial wink. "That boyfriend of yours is in an hour-long meeting, and he won't need me for a hot second. I'll bring it to you. Need to get my steps in anyway."

I smile, genuinely grateful for Sandy, before heading back to my desk. When Sandy brings me the tea, I could melt with gratitude. The subtle spice in the tea tastes delicious, and within minutes my nausea subsides.

It's great because, once I call Monica, I'm feeling on top of the world. No pregnancy symptoms to bring me down. We talk through the new fantasy feature that they're launching which allows the viewer to take a quiz and receive customized content based on their fantasies. I offer my own thoughts and promise to do some mock-ups on what the marketing could look like.

"I knew you were perfect for this," Monica says on the other end of the phone. "A young girl just dipping her toes in the dating pool—you're a dream, Emery!"

I nearly choke on my ginger tea.

"Yep, that's me," I say, hoping I don't sound as false as I feel.

We wrap up quickly, my mind spinning. Just because I'm going to have a baby doesn't mean that I'm not going to be perfect for this job anymore.

Does it?

I decide to look through some of the information that the doctor sent home with me. To my shock and horror, apparently the first trimester is incredibly uncomfortable, and my symptoms are only just starting. Sensitivity to certain foods? Nausea? Vomiting? Swollen breasts? Swollen ankles?

Basically, swollen everything.

Ugh. I knew time was limited, but now I know that it's going to take a hell of a lot to push through this.

And even if I do, will I even have a job to come back to?

I spend the rest of the day alternating between stressing about the pregnancy and stressing about my job, even though stress, according to my doctor, is something I should expressly avoid.

But how am I even supposed to do that with life as I know it hanging on the line?

CHAPTER EIGHT

HARRISON

"I DON'T KNOW what the hell to do."

It started as a work conversation. Ramon and I were in my office talking about Germany and how, apparently, we only have assholes working on that account.

Incompetent assholes who don't know how to deal in foreign affairs.

Incompetent assholes who lack the sensitivity and the know-how to get shit done.

I'd told Ramon that we needed new people on the team. I wasn't about to give anyone an excuse to say that my company did anything half-ass. We were going to fix this, and we were going to do it today. I didn't give a damn if we had to throw together new material in a matter of minutes, if we had to hire new people and put them to work immediately. We were doing it.

Ramon agreed. He'd been on the call with me. He knew I was pissed, rightly so. But I could tell that, once we'd put the Germany issue to bed, he still had something else to say.

"Harrison," he'd said. "How are things going with Emery?"

My eyes had snapped to him. He'd asked with an innocent tone, the most neutral expression possible, one that didn't give anything away. And yet, I knew, with one look, that he knew, like I did, that something was off.

Or maybe he just knew that something was off with me and there was only one reason why I'd be distracted.

Emery.

"She's pregnant," I'd explained, my own tone a bit of a groan because I'm still processing it and also, I don't know how the fuck to handle it, exactly. I mean, there's not much for me to do besides support her and worry about shit.

"What do you mean you don't know what to do?" Ramon asks with a laugh. "Of course you know what to do. You make Emery's life as easy as possible. Whatever she wants to do or not do, you figure it out. You get her prenatal massages. You tell that private chef of yours to make food that'll help her pregnancy symptoms. And when she has a weird craving for Nutella at four in the morning, you go get it."

"Nutella?" I ask. "I take it you're speaking from experience?"

Ramon smiles. "And I didn't have a driver to go get it for me, I'll remind you."

"It's just that she's acting strange," I tell him. "Moody? I don't know. She actually mentioned going back to Kansas. Again."

Ramon's eyes widen. "Why?"

"I don't know," I admit. "Something about her mother. She seemed to think I wouldn't be able to take care of her. It can't be that hard to care for a pregnant woman, surely.

Complete idiots manage it every day," I add a bit sullenly. I run a Fortune 500 company. Surely I can manage this.

"Or," Ramon offers slowly, as if he's talking down a feral cat. "Perhaps she thought you wouldn't want to?"

Hmph.

"That's ridiculous," I snap. "And if that thought even entered her head then it's some kind of pregnancy psychosis. Of course I want to. And I made that clear to her. She's not going anywhere."

"First of all, friend, I'm going to give you your first piece of parental advice." Ramon levels me a look as he places his hands firmly on my desk. And I didn't miss that he called me friend, not boss, so clearly Ramon is not going to sugar coat this for me.

"Go on," I prod.

"Whatever you do, do not, under any circumstances, repeat the words *pregnancy psychosis* to Emery."

I nod. That's solid advice.

"I'm not done." Ramon shakes his head like I'm some kind of idiot, and then I swear to God, he lowers his voice like Anita might overhear him from fucking Brooklyn. "Not a word about hormones or mood swings and do not be that guy that tells her you know how she feels. It's a trap. You don't know how she feels. You can't know. Don't go there." Ramon shakes his head again as he sits back down.

"Okay, okay. I got it. I'll tread delicately."

"Now," Ramon continues, "let's circle back to how you made it clear to Emery, that you're excited about the baby, that you love her, and that you're going to do whatever it takes to make her happy?"

I stiffen. "Well, I didn't make some Disney prince speech about it, but I made it clear."

Ramon just shakes his head. "Harrison, you might want to throw on a romance every once in a while. Or a rom-com, even."

I roll my eyes. "Emery knows that we're serious. That I'm serious about her. I flew to Kansas to woo her back to New York with me, didn't I?"

"Which was very romantic," Ramon agrees. "But the romance can't stop now. Especially not when she's pregnant."

I consider whether or not to reveal the next tidbit, and then, because Ramon is looking at me like I'm a kid who doesn't understand a math problem, I give in and tell him.

"I'm planning to propose," I say. "Soon."

Ramon grins. "Well, that's great. I'm sure that'll show Emery that you're serious."

"Of course," I say, feeling pleased.

"How are you going to do it?"

"For fuck's sake, you fucking girl. Does it matter? I'm going to propose, that's the important part. There's a ring, there's a question, there's a yes. Jesus."

I think I liked Ramon better when he didn't insist on schooling me about feelings and shit.

Ramon raises an eyebrow. "You sure about that?"

"I'll figure it out," I say. "I know Emery. I'll figure it out."

My carriage plan might have been a disaster, but this won't be. A proposal will take away all of Emery's concerns in one fell swoop.

"Well, she can talk to Anita any time," Ramon offers.

"About the pregnancy. They get easier with each one. Plus, we can tell you what you'll need."

Oh fuck that.

"You're probably not supposed to know yet," I admit. "So pretend you don't know for now. Honestly, I wouldn't have told you if you didn't insist on all this talking."

"Already forgotten," Ramon says, holding up his hands.

After that, we get back to some of the other accounts, and it feels good to lose myself for a bit in numbers and facts. What's going on with Emery feels so out of my hands, but that'll all be taken care of once I've proposed. We'll be on the same page then.

The rest of the day passes in a blur. More meetings, more calls, more things to fix. The nervous energy from before creeps back in, and I know I'm going to have to do something to beat it back into submission.

I let Emery know that I'm going for a run after work. I need to clear my head, but more than that, I need to get into a very particular headspace. I change into my running clothes and leave my suit with Sandy for the dry cleaners, and then I head out, pounding the sidewalks of New York.

The run is one that I've done thousands of times. I head down the street, past the other businesses and restaurants, down to Central Park. The air's clean tonight, and the sky's dotted with only a few clouds. With each pump of my arms and my legs, I feel everything coming together for the next part of my plan. Ramon's words just cemented it for me, and I know now, more than anything, that I'm making the right decision.

Emery and I belong together, after all. From the moment when she spilled coffee on me, there was a spark.

But how was I supposed to know that that spark would ignite a fire that would pull me back into believing in love?

Not just believing in it, but falling head over ass for it.

I'd thought for so long that Blythe had ruined any belief in love for me. I looked out at this city and I saw gray buildings and gray futures, but now, I see the city the way Emery does. As a place of possibility. A place of promise.

Back when Duke Capital had just started to grow, I did this run probably a hundred times, looking at the building that I was considering for my business. It took months to build it up to the point where we could even think about moving, but the entire time, I saw the vision. I saw the skyscraper with the letters spelling "Duke Capital" spread out across the top.

Words that could be seen and read for miles.

A business that would one day be envied and coveted.

A dream that I realized and achieved with nothing but my own vision.

It's a vision that won't fail me in the future. Just like with my company, I know that the life I'm building for me and Emery will be perfect.

And I know just the way to kick it off.

CHAPTER NINE

EMERY

I'M grateful when Harrison tells me he's going for a run after work because it gives me permission to turn into a complete and total couch potato.

It's one thing to be a couch potato in an apartment where you have to share said couch with roommates, or where you have to put up with them bringing over their newest paramour who has a strong affinity for hemp. But when you live in a place like Harrison's, being a couch potato is the ultimate relaxation. The couch itself is huge and ridiculously comfy, and it faces a TV that might as well be a movie theatre screen.

Plus, now I get to make popcorn all by myself. Popcorn was always a favorite treat for me back at home. Mom and I especially were into it. We'd mix up different toppings for the popcorn or she'd throw in something bizarre like chocolate chips, and we'd rate our favorites as we watched terrible movie after terrible movie. Sometimes, we managed to get a good movie in there, but we were often limited to Mom and Dad's basic DVD collection and whatever the TV happened to be showing at the time. Sometimes, we'd go wild and rent something, but that was rare.

We alternated who got to choose the movie, and Mom could always be counted on to choose something super old and super cheesy. She did show me a few movies that would become my favorites, like *Bringing Up Baby* and *Overboard*, but they were few and far between. More often than not, it was some made-for-TV movie.

Maybe it's being pregnant that's making me reach for nostalgia as a comfort, but all I want right now is something terrible on TV and popcorn that's drenched in butter. With Harrison out running, there's never been a better time to do it. So I pull on my rattiest pajamas, complete with an unattractive stain on the chest from where I once spilled marinara sauce, and head to the kitchen for popcorn.

I won't be able to make it from scratch, but I do find a few bags of popcorn in the back of the cabinet that will do to start. I throw them in one at a time in the microwave and then warm up an entire stick of butter to drizzle over the popcorn.

Next, I go hunting for something that will work in terms of toppings. I have a moment of insane luck when I find a bag of Peanut Butter M&M's. These are the holy grail. Not peanut, which is too crunchy to mix with popcorn, but peanut butter. These will basically melt in with the butter and the popcorn. I take a picture of my final concoction for Mom and text it to her.

Mom: LOL! I'll have to make my own. What's the movie?

Me: Haven't decided yet!

Because tonight the possibilities are endless since

Harrison has every streaming service known to man, linked to the television. I manage to find *Legally Blonde* and decide to let Elle Woods and popcorn lull me into comfort.

The popcorn's delicious, but Elle's barely arrived at Harvard when I feel my lids getting heavy. Working while pregnant's no joke, and I know I'm doomed the first time I nod off. I manage to stay awake long enough to see Elle realize she's been replaced before I nod off again and fall dead asleep right there on the couch.

I dream a perfect dream. Harrison and I are in France where I wear a bikini that shows off perfect abs that I definitely don't have in real life. We stroll down a French beach until we find an open patch of sand, and Harrison kisses me all over until I'm flushed and radiating with pleasure. We see all of the sights, and he twirls me down the cobblestone streets while a man plays a fiddle as he follows us. I drink too much wine but it doesn't matter because, in dreams, you can't get a hangover. We make love on the balcony of our room, looking over the twinkling lights of the city, and nothing could be better. Nothing.

It must be a few hours later when Harrison gently jostles me awake. I smile, eyes still closed. I don't even care that he's found me asleep, clutching a bowl of popcorn, butter no doubt smeared on my face. I'm just so happy he's here.

I'm also probably a little delirious and on a sugar-high, but who cares.

"Emery," Harrison says in that delicious, low voice of his. "Emery, wake up."

My eyes flutter open, and there he is, crouching next to me. He's freshly showered, his thin pajama shirt sticking to his chest. I want to run my hands along it, but I should probably wash the butter off first.

"Emery," he says, and I must still be half in dreamland because the next words he says are, "Marry me."

"Mmm," I say, and then suddenly my eyes fly completely open. "Wait, *what*?"

He's grinning, and I think maybe this is a joke because I look like some terrifying butter gremlin. I yank my hand out of the popcorn and drop the bowl, sending popcorn and M&M's flying everywhere.

Harrison just laughs. "I want to make an honest woman out of you, Emery. Marry me."

For a moment, I just stare at him, still thinking this is a joke until I see the ring. It sparkles in the light of the television, and he holds it out on his hand. Not between his fingers but in his palm, like an afterthought that he picked up the same way someone might pick up their keys.

Oh, for fuck's sake. He's got the guilt because he knocked me up. He won't mean this later. And if I let him go through with it, he'll hate me for it. He'll spend the rest of our lives feeling trapped by me, the same way he felt and still feels trapped by Blythe and the charity.

I refuse to do that to him. I refuse to let him do that to me.

Still, it breaks my heart. Because this means that I was right. He doesn't really want this. He's just doing what he thinks he's supposed to.

I'll have to pull back and give him time to gently extricate himself from me. It's the only way forward for both of us.

I swallow a breath.

"I don't know," I say.

CHAPTER TEN

HARRISON

THE WORDS HIT me like a truck.

"I don't know."

How is that possible? How are those the three words she decides to say? As I was jogging through the streets, all I could imagine was Emery saying "yes."

Yes, she would marry me.

Yes, she wanted to start a life with me.

Yes, she was over the moon that I'd done this incredible and romantic thing for her.

Hell, hadn't Ramon okayed this idea? Hadn't he made it clear that this was what Emery would want and need? Then there's Emery herself, telling me before about needing to go back to Kansas. Clearly, she was craving stability, and here I am, on my knees, giving her exactly that.

Or I guess I'm not exactly on my knees. I'm sitting next to her on the couch with popcorn dropped like little bombs all around us. There are M&M's scattered around, too. I'll need to sweep those up before they start to melt.

I look at Emery, waiting for her to jump up for joy, clap her hands together, and tell me that she was only teasing and *of course* she wants to get married.

But she doesn't. She just stares at me. She's in her pajamas, her hair mussed up from sleeping, and even now, she looks beautiful to me. Tired, but beautiful. Because she's mine, and she's carrying my baby.

But apparently, she doesn't want to marry me.

"What do you mean 'I don't know'?" I ask, thinking that maybe she just needs my prompting to take back this horrible joke of hers.

She bites her lip. She starts to pick up the popcorn and M&M's that she can reach to put back into the bowl. She avoids my eyes as she does it.

"I mean, I don't know that you need to rush into this just because I'm pregnant," she says, still not looking at me, still plucking popcorn from the couch.

I scoff at her. How can she even think that? Pregnancy or not, I thought I'd been clear that I was in this for the long haul. And even if she somehow misunderstood that, I was doing the right thing here. I was doing the thing that was supposed to make her happy. Hell, every girl would be overjoyed for a proposal. Goddamned hormones. Tread lightly.

"Of course it's not because you're pregnant," I insist. "I was going to ask you anyway."

Tears bubble up in her eyes, making me wince.

"Don't say that. You're just making it worse."

Oh fuck. She really doesn't believe me. She really doesn't understand.

"I'm not saying it. I mean it. Do you know how long I've had that ring for?"

She huffs, swiping at her eyes with her palm. Then, she glares at me.

"Was it Blythe's?"

Well. This is confirmed hormonal bullshit.

"Are you crazy?" I sputter, clearly forgetting my vow to tread lightly.

She sits up on the couch.

"Then was it your mom's?"

"No. This is your ring. The one I picked out for you."

But she just shakes her head at me.

"If you had a ring just sitting around, that supposedly isn't a hand-me-down, why didn't you propose already?"

Fuck. I really don't want to bring that night up now. Or ever again. I rub a hand over my face in exasperation. How do I tell her I had a ring in my pocket that night? That I'd planned a dinner and a proposal and then—

And then...everything fell apart when I got to her apartment.

"Because, Emery, I found the check my wife gave you."

And now Emery's crying again. She stands up, still shaking her head.

"And then you decided I wasn't wife material," she says. "I understand. I told you, I'll go back to Kansas."

What? How can she even think that's an option? I made my thoughts on that clear.

"Would you stop saying that?" I say a little sharply, more than a little frustrated. How has this gone so wrong? Why doesn't she understand that I'm putting myself on the damn line here? I'm laying myself bare for fuck's sake.

For a moment, she just looks at me. It's like I'm watching her run through every moment of us together, and at the end, she makes a decision. Then, her face sags, and she rubs her temples with her fingertips.

"You know what? I need to sleep. Let's talk about this tomorrow."

She doesn't give me a chance to respond. She turns on her heels and heads straight for the bedroom, and when she's there, she slams the door shut.

What the fuck? I'm tempted to go after her, to demand an explanation, but I know it's no use. There's no coming back from this, at least, not tonight.

I'm tempted to head down to the gym, but instead, I go downstairs to the library and settle into an Eames chair. Proposing was a solid idea, right? My conversation with Ramon earlier today burns in my mind.

Have you showed her that you love her and that you're going to do whatever it takes to make her happy?

I've said as much, haven't I?

I've proposed.

Does she want me to beg?

I must be missing something.

I thought this would be exactly what she'd want, but after tonight, I'm questioning everything. I search my mind for memories of Kansas, of time in her home and in the barn with her. That damn county fair. All of the locations meant something to Emery. It wasn't the big gesture that mattered, though. It was the fact that I wanted her, and I proved it to her. I went to her doorstep and I won her back.

Harrison, you might want to throw on a romance every once in a while. Or a rom-com, even.

Begrudgingly, and I'm not proud of this, I google the names of some romances and then scroll through their

Wikipedia summaries. There was an entire bookshelf of old rom-com DVDs at Emery's mom's house so this research isn't completely asinine. I might as well know what I'm up against. And there, in every plot, is the big moment. The emotionally charged reveal.

And that, I realize, is where I royally fucked up.

There was nothing personal about my proposal. Hell, Emery was in her damn pajamas and half asleep. It felt like something I was checking off a list because, well, it was.

Of course she deserves better.

How didn't I see it before?

This calls for an entirely new plan. Something that's personal to us. A proposal that would only make sense for my Coffee Girl.

I land on an idea.

An idea so perfect that it will clear every doubt she has about us until the only logical answer will be, yes.

CHAPTER ELEVEN

EMERY

I'VE DECIDED that I really, really, really hate morning sickness.

I'm also not a fan of whoever it was that came up with the term "morning sickness" because my body doesn't seem to be following any specific time. In fact, I think I could handle it if it was just happening in the morning. I could do my time hugging the toilet before the day got started and then leave and focus on the rest of my life.

But it doesn't work like that.

Sure, it starts in the morning. It starts with me waking up feeling nauseous and aching and just plain sick. And then I empty my stomach, and if that was it, then I could deal with it. But the horrible part is the lingering. Not to mention, barfing into random toilets. Ew.

All day, I feel sick. I teeter on the edge of another race to the restroom, and no amount of ginger teas or chews seems to make a difference. At least not a big difference. Instead, I live in a constant state of either "currently experiencing" morning sickness or "still recovering from" morning sickness.

Harrison watches me like a hawk now, always waiting to see if there's something I need. He's the one who actually found a brand of ginger chews that sort of help, at least, a little. For the past week, he's thrown himself into research for me and the baby, reading things like how I need to have a "rainbow" of fruits and veggies available to me for my diet. He also likes to tell me how big the baby is. Currently, it's the size of a raspberry.

Part of me wishes he wasn't acting this way. I know it's all out of guilt, just like the marriage proposal. He hasn't mentioned it again, probably because he wants to take it back. Which I can't really blame him for. At least he's committed to being my baby daddy, and I can't ask for anything else.

I *have* tried to pull back from him. I've tried to make it so that it will be easier for both of us when this is over. But it's damn hard when he's there telling me that he's having a special tea shipped in from Germany because some pregnancy expert recommended it.

It's hard when he keeps being…nice.

When I start romanticizing how wonderful he's being, I remind myself that, if I let him trap himself into a quick marriage, he'll resent me forever. He'll resent me and our baby, and the forced insta-family and I could never let that happen. So I try, really, to make it less obvious how completely head over heels I am for him.

Then, he catches me in a before-work kiss, and I lose all willpower immediately.

Thankfully, my body seems to be on board with my

distance plan, even if I'm not. My nausea's been the world's biggest cock block, popping up at the most inconvenient times possible.

But I guess it's what I need, seeing as I have no self-control whatsoever when it comes to Harrison Duke.

"How're you feeling?"

I look up from the paper. At first I thought an actual paper was pretty old school, but now I'm charmed by it. There's something soothing about turning the pages I've slipped away from Harrison. I've even started doing the crossword. It helps me settle my brain while I work on settling my stomach in the mornings.

Harrison's standing there, his T-shirt clinging to his chest after his morning run. He's clearly worked up quite a sweat, and I bite my lip, thinking about following him into the shower even though I already took one.

At the thought of wanting to jump Harrison's bones, I wait for my traitorous stomach to object, but for the first time all week, it doesn't. In fact, I feel...good?

It takes me off guard. I've felt like a prisoner in my body lately, waiting at the mercy of whatever it will decide is its newest trigger, but instead, I feel like I could go hop on Harrison's treadmill and run a few miles of my own.

Okay, maybe not that good, but I never feel like doing that.

I do feel like I could go do my cardio class, at least.

"I feel great, actually," I say. "Like...really, really great."

Immediately, Harrison's face brightens. He walks over and kneels next to me, eyes darting to my stomach. I'm not showing or anything, but we both know that's where our raspberry-sized baby is growing.

"Really?" Harrison asks. "You're feeling okay?"

"Better than okay," I say. "I feel amazing."

Harrison grins. "Well then. Do you think you might be up for an adventure today?"

Immediately, I feel something electric slide through me. It's a Saturday, and I've basically been trapped in either the office or this place all week. And, as incredible as Harrison's place is, I've still been itching to get outside. And now that my body doesn't feel hell-bent on betraying me, I'm raring to go.

"Okay," I agree. "What'd you have in mind?'

His grin widens as he stands up. "Well, I was thinking about how we haven't completed your list of New York tourist traps."

"Oh?"

He nods. "What do you think? Want to be a tourist again?"

I consider this. "Do I get to know where?"

He laughs. "I was thinking it could be a surprise."

"Well, let's go," I say, standing up and folding the newspaper. "I'm ready!"

He glances at my robe and smiles.

"I'm almost ready," I say. "Just give me a minute."

"We need to wait a bit," he tells me. "I need to make some calls, and besides...I have something else planned for you first."

"Mr. Duke, you're being very mysterious," I say.

"I promise, it's related," he says. "Trust me, Kansas."

I roll my eyes at the nickname but can't help but feel warm. Even if I'm supposed to be pushing him away, he makes it damn difficult when he's like this.

"Bruce is waiting for you downstairs, as soon as you're ready. I'll see you later on this afternoon."

He presses a kiss to my lips, and I wish he would linger. But he doesn't. He gives me a wink, and then he's walking out of the room as he pulls out his phone. He disappears around the corner, and I hear his office door shut.

I sigh. I guess there's nothing to do but head downstairs. I dress quickly, mostly for comfort since I have no idea what awaits me. Downstairs, Bruce is waiting for me with the car door open, but he's completely rigid and won't tell me anything about where Harrison's sending me. Instead, I have to spend the car ride stuck in my own thoughts. All week, I've been so miserable physically that I've pushed all of the emotional stuff to the back of my mind. But now, here it is, ready and willing to be dissected.

But I don't want to dissect it. Not now. For today, I want to enjoy feeling good in all ways. I want to push all my worries aside and pretend that I don't know that happiness has an expiration date. I want to just enjoy being Harrison's girlfriend.

I bite my lip, decision made. For today, I'll just enjoy whatever it is that Harrison has planned. Especially if this is one of the last times I get to have this.

"We're here, Ms. Mills."

I was so lost in my thoughts that I forgot to look out the window, but now, I peek outside. We're outside a high-end spa. It looks like some sort of oasis, right in the middle of Manhattan. Boxed hedges line the sidewalk of one of the most beautiful buildings I've ever seen. And along the top, in neat, white font, are the words "Serenity Luxury Spa."

"He sent me to a spa?" I ask Bruce, eyes wide.

"The best spa in New York," Bruce tells me.

I'm at a loss for words looking at the exterior. Because I've never been to a spa, and definitely not one this nice. The closest I've been is to a nail place in the city that Mom and I went to before prom and before weddings. At that place, there were only a couple of ladies who did the mani-pedis and they only had ten different colors, all of which were basically pink, red, or peach. This place looks like it's hiding a palace inside, complete with magical fairy-tale garden.

I step out of the car and am immediately greeted by a kind-faced woman who walks me inside. The sound of water trickling through a fountain along with calming spa music plays in the background while she shows me a menu of my options. They've got manicures and pedi-cures, but they also have facials, massages, spa treatments, mud baths, and more.

"Mr. Duke booked you for a facial, prenatal massage, and a manicure-pedicure to start with," the woman tells me. "I would also recommend some of our other prenatal services. They're a lifesaver for first trimester symptoms."

I jolt a little at this stranger knowing that I'm pregnant, especially when my own mom still doesn't know, but she smiles as if reading my mind.

"We are very discreet, Ms. Mills," she assures me. "I only mention it because our goal today—and Mr. Duke's goal—is to help you feel your very best. You deserve that."

I deserve that.

Do I?

In Kansas, the extent of my self-care was throwing on some face masks that I got at the drug store, and I haven't exactly expanded my repertoire here in New York. But even though I woke up feeling better today, I'm desperate to hold on to the feeling. I tell the woman I'll do whatever she recommends, and then, I'm whisked off to a room for my first service.

My facial starts with a technician gently massaging my face and neck as she cleanses my skin with a gritty but cooling exfoliant. The smells are out of this world, rich and heady like eucalyptus. She reminds me as she's working her fingers over the sides of my face to unclench my jaw, and that's when I realize just how much stress I've been holding in.

Falling in love with Harrison was a whirlwind. Getting my dream job was a whirlwind. Finding out I was having a baby? That was basically a tornado, and I haven't exactly come up for air.

But she's right. I've been holding so much in, and as the minutes pass, I feel some of the stress leaving me. I feel like I'm getting back to me.

From there, it's one wonderful treatment after another. The prenatal massage in particular is divine, relaxing muscles that I didn't even realize I had. My feet and hands emerge from the manicure-pedicure feeling softer than they've ever been in my life and painted a soft pink.

It's a little bit like being reborn, I decide. Somebody goes in and scuffs off all of the tension and pressure, and for the first time since I sat in that OB/GYN's office surrounded by photos of pregnant women, I can actually, truly breathe.

After the last of my treatments, I'm led to a glass atrium garden for meditation and tea. I'm surrounded by the smell of star jasmine flowers as I sip the tea, and as I breathe it all in, I make a decision.

I'm allowed to enjoy the rest of today.

I deserve to enjoy the rest of today.

But after that, it has to stop.

I can't afford to take any more from Harrison.

I have to do the rest of this on my own.

———

MY NEXT STOP is at a boutique. Harrison's pre-arranged a personal shopper who greets me with a fitting room already decked out with options in my size. The saleswoman flutters around like a magical butterfly, showing me all my options for tonight. I try to use the outfits to gauge where Harrison might be taking me. The dresses are certainly luxurious, made of beautiful jewel-toned fabrics that I absolutely adore, but they're not black-tie fancy. Best of all, they're comfortable and feel heavenly against my skin.

I decide on a pale peach dress that skims my curves and pairs beautifully with a jade necklace the saleswoman happily places around my neck. It's dainty and hangs from a long gold chain. My hair and makeup were done at the spa, nothing overdone, natural tones and my hair tied back in a fancy version of a low pony. Looking at my reflection now, I look for clues about where we might be going. Dressed up, in an effortlessly casual, highly polished way. I still look like me. A very pretty version of me, but still me.

Maybe we're going back to a museum, I think. One of the

famous ones. Or one of the restaurants that's run by a famous chef. This is definitely a date outfit, after all.

I thank my fairy saleswoman profusely. Feeling waited on is still so weird to me, but tonight, I'm trying to accept it all. Soon, it will be nothing but a happy memory.

Don't think about that, I tell myself. *Stay in the moment.*

Bruce and I head back to the car, and then we're off, whirring down the street. I try to keep track of where we're going, but I still don't know New York that well. I'm lost in a sea of concrete for a while until, at last, I start to recognize some places.

Then, I see it.

A towering building with gorgeous art deco design and windows.

The iconic sculpture at the center.

Rockefeller Center.

It's been in countless movies that I've loved ever since I was a kid, but up close, it looks…magical. There's no other way to describe it. When Harrison and I came here before, I was like a little girl in a candy store. We went on the tour and I memorized all of the facts about the incredible art deco pieces. It was definitely one of my favorites, but we already did this and Harrison said we were doing something new. Unless he's already forgotten?

I look for him now. People fill the space, moving in a rhythm around the front of the building, but my eyes stick on one person standing on the sidewalk, looking right at me.

Harrison, waiting for me in his suit.

As soon as I'm close enough not to be overly dramatic I run the last few steps between us and throw my arms around his neck. He scoops me up and kisses me, and he tastes like mints and maybe a hint of whiskey. I could get lost in his lips, in the soft way they move against mine, welcoming me back. He smiles against my mouth and chuckles.

"I take it you liked the spa?"

I grin, pulling back to look at him. "I could get used to that."

"I can make that happen," he promises, kissing my forehead.

"But Harrison..." I say, looking around at Rockefeller. "Why are we here? I thought you said we were going somewhere new."

He smiles and hooks his arm in mine. "Trust the process, Kansas."

I roll my eyes but my heart jumps. Ever since he kissed me, I've felt like I was floating.

He reads my expression and pauses. "You're still feeling okay?"

I nod. "Like a million spa dollars."

His smile broadens. "Excellent. Then follow me."

We head into the Grand Atrium lobby, and immediately, my breath catches. High above us, casting a glittering glow across the entire interior of the building, is the largest chandelier I've ever seen.

"Her name's Joie," an employee to my left says, grinning.

"I beg your pardon?" I ask, and Harrison snorts next to me.

"The chandelier," the guy clarifies. "It's called the Joie Chandelier. Made up of 14,000 crystals and made by Swarovski just for us."

"Oh," I say, feeling dumb. "She's beautiful."

"So are you," Harrison whispers into my ear, and then he turns to the guy. "Are you Don?"

The guy—Don—nods. "Yes, Mr. Duke. I'm ready to take you up."

I cast Harrison a questioning look, but he just shrugs innocently. We follow Don over to an elevator, and he gestures for us to step inside. I do, but Harrison lingers next to Don.

"Have all of the proper arrangements been made?" Harrison asks.

Don nods and smiles, glancing at me.

"Yes, sir."

Harrison reaches out and shakes Don's hand, and something tells me that there was probably a wad of cash in that hand.

"What was that about?" I ask.

"Nothing," he says. "Now, are you ready to see the Top of the Rock?"

Did I hear him right? Did he just say Top of the Rock? If Top of the Rock is where we're going, then tonight is really going to be a dream. Top of the Rock is said to have some of the best views in New York City, showing the Empire State Building, the Brooklyn Bridge, Central Park, and more. It was definitely starred in my guidebook.

I practically bounce on my feet. "Yes!"

We fly up seventy stories, my stomach flipping the entire time—but this time, thank God, it's not because of morning sickness. It's pure excitement bubbling through me.

As soon as we hit the top, I'm nearly beside myself with excitement, and Harrison has to take my hand to keep me from sprinting off the elevator.

"Harrison, hurry!" I say. "It's almost sundown, and my guidebook always said that that's the perfect time for photos. It's going to be crowded, so we better—"

"It's not going to be crowded," he tells me, tugging me closer with a smile. "I bought out the space."

I tilt my head back to get a better look at him, sure I've misunderstood. "What?"

"We have a private viewing," he tells me. "So we can take our time."

"Oh," I say, eyes widening. "Well, still, we don't want to miss the sunset."

"I'll buy every sunset for you," he says with a sexy grin and I nearly stumble because something sticks inside of me at those words, and I pause standing in the elevator. Harrison's smile is soft against his hard jaw, and he's looking at me like I'm something precious. It breaks my heart to know that this won't be forever. That I'm going to have to leave him and New York behind.

But at least I'll have tonight. This memory.

I turn and head out of the elevator, enjoying the incredible view of New York City in all of its glory. The sun's casting a soft orange glow over all of the buildings, and their windows are twinkling in the dying light.

But it's not just the Top of the Rock view. There are flower petals everywhere I walk, and when I get further out from the elevator, there's the sound of a saxophone drifting through the air. I turn the final corner until I'm exposed to the entire Top of the Rock world, and I spot the saxophone player in the flesh. He gives me a friendly wave and returns to playing his music. I'm so mesmerized by him, by the flower petals, by New York all around me, that I don't hear Harrison come up behind me until he says my name.

"Emery."

I spin around, and there he is, standing and smiling at me.

"Emery," he repeats. "I brought you here because I need you to believe me when I tell you that this is your home. That you won't ever have to leave here again. Because when I make a promise to you, I won't ever go back on it. And I'm promising you that you belong here. In this city. With me. Forever."

Oh my God. Oh my God. Is he saying what I think he's saying? Is he—

"I love the way you look at this city," he continues, "how you look at life. Like it's an endless opportunity…" He pauses, looking around us at the views of the New York City skyline. "As a place of hope. I'd forgotten to look at this city that way. Hell, I'd forgotten to look at people that way. But you reminded me that this world is good. That I can be a good man within it. As long as you're by my side."

I gasp as he drops to his knees and pulls a box out of his pocket. When he flips it open, the ring inside glitters, throwing its shimmers all around me with the help of the sun's final rays.

"I wanted to tell you before," Harrison continues. "I wanted you to know that *you* are my home, Emery Mills. Wherever you are, I'll be there. I'll spend the rest of my life making you happy, if you'll let me.

"I'll be a good husband, Emery. A good father to our children. I'll prove it to you. Just say you'll marry me and give me the chance."

All of my fears, all of my worries, all of it evaporates at the look on Harrison's face. At the sincerity there. Because I believe him.

This moment was everything I ever wanted, and he cared enough to make sure I had it.

"Yes," I say, the world tumbling out of my mouth. "Oh my God, yes."

CHAPTER TWELVE

HARRISON

SHE SAID YES.

For a moment, I can't believe it. Because not for nothing, I can still visualize her back at my place shaking her head and saying "I don't know" as she avoided looking at me. But then I blink and I'm back here, on Top of the Rock, and she's giddy and grinning as I slide the ring onto her finger.

It looks perfect on her. Fucking perfect as it glitters on top of the world.

"It's beautiful," she whispers, shifting her hand back and forth as she stares down at it. Then, she looks up at me, and I see that she's tearing up. "All of this was beautiful, Harrison."

I can't help it. I'm grinning like a total idiot because I'm proud as hell of what I pulled off. Because as long as I've know her, I've known Emery's a romantic. Looking at New York like it was some kind of a dream come true, looking at me like I actually had happily ever after potential. I was a fool for fucking it up in the first place, but I fixed it.

Of course, the location was the easy part. Figuring out that Top of the Rock was the place to give her, well, her own rock, didn't take long.

But figuring out what to say?

Forcing myself to be "emotionally vulnerable," as Ramon had suggested before I'd shot him a look to kill.

That was trickier.

"You have to be honest with her," Ramon had said. "Just tell her everything she means to you, and you'll be fine."

Not that I'd been asking Ramon for advice, exactly. More like, I brought it up to pick his brain a little bit. Which is just smart. I'd fucked it up so much the first time that I didn't have much of a choice. His advice was easy enough to follow in theory, but in actuality? I wasn't sure I could pull it off.

But once I saw Emery in that elevator tonight, I knew that the stakes were too high for me to *not* swing for the fences. I knew she still hadn't been convinced that I was all in on the baby and all in on her—on us. The whole week, she'd been closed off. And I knew that I needed to lay it all on the line.

Waiting had been another pain in my ass, but it was necessary. I knew I couldn't go into another proposal with Emery feeling like shit, emotionally and physically, so I bided my time. Thank God it only took a week. Just enough time for her to realize I was serious and not giving up on our forever.

And it worked.

She said yes.

She's in front of me wearing the engagement ring. The ring that says to the rest of the world that she's mine. Forever.

I step closer to her and run my fingertip along her jaw, tilting her chin up so that she's looking into my eyes. There's a lifetime of promise in those eyes as they look back at me, but there's something else there, too.

Want.

Desire.

For me.

I turn my head to find the saxophone player, but he must have made his graceful exit already because there's no one in sight.

I pull Emery against me, and her lips meet mine with hunger. I press against her, letting her feel just how much my cock wants her right now. She moans at the touch, and I slip my tongue between her lips, tasting how sweet she is.

My fiancée.

The woman who's going to be my wife.

I kiss down her jaw and then to her neck, and she shivers against me, fisting her hands in my jacket.

"Don't do that," she says, giggling against me as she pulls back. "I don't need security coming up here to break us up."

I quirk an eyebrow. "So you're saying you can't resist me?"

She nips at my lip. "You know I can't."

"Then we should get going," I tell her. "I've reserved the top floor of the St. Regis to continue with your New York education tonight."

She stares at me. "You didn't."

I smile. "Of course I did. And there should be sparkling cider and strawberries waiting for us."

"Cider, huh? You thought of everything."

"I did," I agree, leaning in to nip at her ear. "And I can't wait to show you." I grind against her to make my point, and she gasps. Her eyes darken with lust.

"Then we better not waste any time."

———

THE REST of the weekend passes in a beautiful blur of sex and celebration. We fuck with abandon, and the sight of Emery's fingers encircling my dick—that diamond ring sparkling on top of them—sticks with me even after we've passed out from our respective orgasms. While she sleeps, I watch her and repeat to myself, over and over again, that she said yes.

That she's going to marry me.

That she's the future Mrs. Duke.

The forever Mrs. Duke.

On Monday, it's back to reality and to work, and Emery's morning sickness decides to make a reappearance. But she swears up and down that it isn't as bad as before, and she's hopeful that this is just one final kick in the ass before it's gone for good.

"I'll be fine," she promises as we hop in the car to head to work. "I feel better already, I swear."

She tucks a hair behind her ear with one hand while she searches in her purse for lipstick with the other. We're running a bit late thanks to the morning sickness, but she should know it doesn't matter. I'm the goddamn CEO, after all.

But the movement catches my eye for another reason. The ring that I've gotten so used to seeing this weekend isn't there. My stomach drops. Is she having second thoughts?

Emery catches me looking and waves her hand out, showing me that she is actually wearing the ring—but it's turned inside to her palm so that it just looks like a band from the outside.

"I'm trying to be inconspicuous," she says. "We don't need everyone at work knowing."

"And why not?" I ask. "Sandy's going to be thrilled. And Ramon—"

"They're fine," she says. "They're our friends. But I mean the rest of the company. Can't we just keep it a secret for now?"

She looks at me with those big doe eyes, and I sigh. "Fine," I say, though I don't understand it. No need to pressure her into telling everyone. But she should be thrilled, shouldn't she? Aren't most newly engaged women acting like their hands are too heavy just for an excuse to show off their rings? Hell, Blythe certainly didn't miss an opportunity to flash her ring around in front of everyone's faces.

But that's just it, of course. Emery isn't like those girls, and she certainly isn't like Blythe. And besides, there will be plenty of time to celebrate later. I can relax for now. I do have work to do today, after all.

But then we're walking into the office, and Sandy's there ready to take my coat, and I can't help it. The words just spill out.

"Emery and I are engaged," I tell her, and Sandy lets out a squeal.

"Oh how wonderful! You're so good for him," Sandy says, grabbing Emery's hand to see the ring. Emery blushes but doesn't look too furious with me. And she did say Sandy was allowed to know, didn't she?

"Keep it down," Emery says with a laugh. "God, Harrison, way to keep a secret."

"Is it a secret?" Sandy says, looking between us. "Well, it'll be hard to keep with a rock like that. But I'm thrilled for you anyway."

"Just trying to keep it on the DL," Emery says, rolling her eyes. "We're excited, but…"

I wait for the reason, but she can't seem to find one.

"We're telling work friends," I say to Sandy. "Just not the entire company."

Sandy makes a motion like she's zipping her lips. Then, my phone rings, and she waves us off.

Emery flips on me the second we're in my office.

"We literally just talked about this!"

"And you said Sandy was okay," I point out. "And Ramon."

"Yes, but Harrison, I haven't even told my family," she says. "Can't we just wait a little?"

Ah. Well, there it is.

And she's right, after all.

In all my excitement, I forgot that there is a world beyond her and me.

"You're right, of course," I say, taking her hands. I run my thumb over her palm. "I'm sorry."

"It's okay," she says. "Just…simmer down, okay? We've both got a lot of work to do today, anyway."

"You're right," I repeat, nodding. "Especially since we'll be leaving for Connecticut this weekend."

Emery blinks at me. "What? Why?"

I stare at her. I could've sworn I mentioned this yesterday in between fucking her senseless.

"Connecticut," I repeat. "Remember? To see Dad and Mom Number Three? Time to meet my family, now that we're engaged."

Emery just stares at me. "Your dad. And Mom Number Three. What…what happened to Mom Number Two?" she asks.

Sigh. She should know, of course. What happens to most marriages.

"Eh, the usual," I say.

She makes a face, but it's one I can't quite figure out. Then, she covers her mouth, and I know that her morning sickness has reappeared and she'll be making a run for the bathroom soon.

"We'll talk more at lunch," I tell her, and she nods and turns, rushing out of the room.

It reminds me that we're actually juggling two secrets: our engagement and Emery's pregnancy.

And one of them won't be quite as easy to hide.

CHAPTER THIRTEEN

EMERY

"EH. THE USUAL."

The words run through my head for the rest of the week, but somehow, I can't get up the courage to ask what the heck "the usual" is.

I mean, obviously, it's divorce. There's nothing else that "the usual" would be. And it's not like I'm a stranger to the concept. There're my own parents and then there're Harrison and Blythe. I know it exists. That's not what has me shaken and circling that sentence again and again.

No.

It was the casual flippancy in how Harrison said it, as if it's normal or even expected for a marriage to end in divorce.

Not a big deal.

But he can't actually believe that, can he? Otherwise, he would've never proposed to me. He would've eschewed marriage altogether because what would even be the point?

Right?

I touch my stomach. I was so sure, in the moment, that Harrison proposed because he truly and completely loved me, that it didn't have to do with guilt or the fact that I'm pregnant. And I still believe that. I know he loves me. I know he wants to marry me.

But is he going into it expecting it might end one day?

I decide that this has to be the pregnancy hormones and that I'm just overthinking. It was a throwaway comment, and it doesn't line up at all with his enthusiasm for our engagement. Heck, if anything, he's *too* enthusiastic about our engagement. He's the one eagerly telling anyone who will listen. Colleagues, the doorman, a waiter. No matter how many times I tell him to cool it, somehow, it just slips out. First, it was Sandy, then Ramon, then Bethany, and then, suddenly, it was some random IT worker who came in to fix the Wi-Fi in Harrison's office.

"What?" Harrison said after the guy left, polite but clearly confused. "I thought you two were close."

With him this excited, I'm able to sort of quiet the part of me that's still semi-worried that he only proposed out of guilt. It's clear that he sees a future together, and I have to believe that it's a lifetime future, not a pit stop on his way to Wife Number 3.

I have to believe that or I'll go out of my mind.

Plus, I have plenty of other things to focus on. Like work projects and the endless streams of Pinterest boards my mother has been making now that all her motherly and grandmotherly dreams are coming true at once. Like getting ready to meet his family in Connecticut. I'm grateful that my morning sickness seems to have subsided again. At my checkup with my doctor, she was hopeful that I might be through the worst of it. All I can do is hope for the best, especially since I'm about to meet the parents.

Or, at least, his Dad and "Mom Number Three," who I have since learned are named Paul and Genevieve. But other than their names, Harrison wasn't super forthcoming about their personalities. He tells me that they're "typical East Coast people," which honestly, doesn't mean anything. The only exciting tidbit he does give me is that, apparently, they live on a farm. With horses! So at least we'll have that in common to talk about.

However, as we leave the city behind us for Connecticut, I get an immediate "we're not in Kansas anymore vibe." Because what we're approaching is most definitely not a farm.

"Why did you lie to me?" I ask, staring open-mouthed out the window. "That giant *mansion* is not a farm!"

Harrison scrunches up his nose. "Yes it is. It's a gentleman's farm, but it's a farm."

"A 'gentleman's farm'?" I say, snorting. "You can't just make stuff up, Harrison."

"If I may," Leo pipes in from the front, "I can confirm that Mr. Duke is correct. The property is a gentleman's farm. It's forty-seven acres."

Now, my mouth really does drop open. Forty. Seven. Acres?

"Including full equestrian facilities," he adds with a happy smile.

Harrison sees my face and just laughs.

"Lunch has been prepared for you in the main house," Leo announces as the car comes to a stop outside a massive front door. "Though it's a bit of a shame, considering how fine the weather is."

I bite my lip and stare at Harrison. He's glancing at his phone, not really paying attention to how weird any of this is. Likely because this world is normal to him.

The main house is so massive I can't even take it all in from the driveway. I suspect the square footage is larger than a superstore, which, considering the fact that it's just two people living here, seems excessive. I think of Mom in her tiny house next to the barn, and I feel a little dizzy.

Harrison grew up here. How is that even possible?

Once we pull up, I follow Harrison quietly into the enormous house. It's all stone and stucco, there's even a couple of turrets, like the entire thing was plucked out of a fairy tale. A fairy tale involving a very expensive architect and building team. I can barely breathe knowing I'm about to meet the most important people in Harrison's life.

What if they hate me?

What if they think I'm not good enough for him?

Me, the farm girl from Kansas.

The Soon-to-Be Wife-Number-Two.

The much younger, wife number two. Am I a cliché trophy wife?

I gulp, but then I feel Harrison's hand on mine, and I'm steadier. Not steady. But steadier.

"Harrison!"

A high-pitched voice echoes through the giant foyer, and I turn to see a brunette-haired woman who might be fifteen years older than me. She's certainly younger than the salt-and-pepper-haired guy standing next to her, who must be Harrison's father, Paul. He's almost as tall as Harrison, with the same sharp jaw and piercing eyes. His wife rushes forward, her many bracelets jingling, and she immediately scoops me up into a crushing hug. Her perfume is so strong that for a terrifying moment I think it's going to make me nauseous, but then she pulls back and the danger passes.

"You must be Emery," she trills. "I'm Genevieve, and I'm just so happy you're both here!"

I smile. "It's nice to meet you, Genevieve. Thank you for having us."

Genevieve claps her hands together, grinning broadly. One look at her face tells me that Genevieve is on a singular mission, and that mission is not to age. Her face is perfect porcelain, not a single line anywhere on her forehead or near her eyes. Her long eyelashes flutter, drawing my attention to the fact that every feature on her face is perfectly proportioned and sized. She must have been a model at some point because her beauty is almost too intense, too shiny and expertly honed. But she seems genuinely warm, so I decide to give her a chance.

"Aren't you just cute as a button?" Genevieve says. "I love your hair color. You'll have to tell me what salon you're using."

"Huh?" I say, and then I realize she's asking for how to get my color. "Oh, this is natural."

"Oh, you lucky little devil," Genevieve says, playfully slapping me on the shoulder. "Well, it's gorgeous. And it falls in such a pretty way. You'll have to wear it down for the wedding."

The blush immediately blooms on my cheeks. Of course, Harrison told them why we were coming. But it still catches me off guard, especially when Genevieve snatches my hand to examine my ring finger.

"Perfect," she says with a little gasp. "Just perfect. But I wouldn't expect anything less from Harrison."

She looks up and winks, and I do my best to smile.

Next to me, Harrison and his father shake hands, and then Paul turns his gaze on me. It's clear that he's appraising me. And unfortunately, he's not nearly as forthcoming with his emotions as his wife. I definitely don't think the words "cute as a button" have ever come out of this man's mouth.

"Emery," he says instead.

And then he nods.

And then he turns and walks away.

"Well, as usual, my hubby's got the right idea!" Genevieve chirps. "Time for lunch, right? You two must be exhausted from the drive in."

Harrison chuckles. "Ginny, it's a ninety-minute drive."

Genevieve shrugs. "Still. Come on!"

She waves us to the dining room. The table's clearly built to fit ten or twelve people, so we all sit on one end, with Paul at the head of the table, Harrison and me to his left, and Genevieve to the right. I look to my plate and find that there are several different forks and knives, but luckily, I thought this might be a thing, so I researched on YouTube. I pick up my salad fork just as a plate of greens is placed in front of me.

Still, as I'm munching on the salad and listening to Genevieve talk about the history of the mansion, I can't help but think about the difference between this place and my home. Mom would've made us a lunch, and it probably would've been a casserole. The forks and knives wouldn't match. There might've been a chip in the casserole dish. And there'd be real farm animals outside, crowing and nickering and demanding attention.

Still, Genevieve's nice, and even if Paul's still just

staring at me without saying anything, I can make small talk. Every Kansas girl can make small talk.

"So, Harrison tells me that you have horses," I say with a big smile. "I grew up riding."

"Oh, did you?" Genevieve says. "How sweet. Competitive show jumping?"

"Oh, no. Just," I falter. *Just regular riding around the farm*, I think to myself, but somehow, I don't really want to say that out loud.

"We take in retired horses," Genevieve adds when I don't elaborate.

"Awww, rescues! I love that!" I say, flashing a relieved grin. "Can I feed them apples after lunch?"

Genevieve's smile falters a bit as she looks at Paul. "Oh, I don't know. We've never done that before. Paul, can the horses have apples?"

I stare at her. Can horses have apples? Is she confused?

Paul shrugs. "I'd have to ask Jeremy. He takes care of them."

"Oh," I say. "Well, that's okay. It'd be great just to see them. How many do you have?"

"Seven," Paul says.

"Wow!" I say. "Do you ride them all?"

Paul stares at me as if my question is obviously stupid.

"Dad doesn't really ride much anymore," Harrison says.

"Right." I nod. "Well, when you did, did you ride Western or English?"

Paul just shrugs. I exchange a glance with Harrison. I'm really trying here, but I'm getting the sense that these people don't actually...do anything with these horses. I bet they've never even mucked a stall.

"Well, I can't wait to see them," I say. "And maybe ride one of them, if possible."

"I'm sure they'd love that!" Genevieve says. "I'm too scared to ride myself, but Firenze Flamethrower's beautiful, and so is Free Drop Tilly. I just love to look at them."

I blink at her. "Sorry, what did you say their names were?"

"Firenze Flamethrower and Free Drop Tilly," Genevieve says, puffing up with pride. "They were my engagement presents from Paul. Both of them won the Derby a few years ago. Not the same year, obviously, but you know what I mean."

Wait. "They won the...Kentucky Derby?"

"Of course," Genevieve says, rubbing Paul's arm. "Paul wanted to give me winners, didn't you, honey?"

Next to me, I swear Harrison chokes on part of his salad.

"Anyway, enough about horses," Genevieve says, waving her hands as the entrées arrive. "Let's talk wedding plans!"

I take a sip of my water and glance at Harrison for guidance or emotional support, or something. This woman has to know that *we* haven't even talked wedding plans yet, right?

"I've got just the best planner," Genevieve says. "She's incredible. She'll get you any venue you want. Anywhere. Honestly, she swears she got a friend of mine the Eiffel Tower. Like, she gets the impossible done. I swear to God."

I bite my lip. "Wow."

"Right?" Genevieve says. "And she takes care of it all. Trust me, when you've got five hundred guests you want someone competent handling it."

My eyes widen. Does she think we're inviting the entire East Coast? "Oh, I don't think we'd have five hundred people... I always envisioned sort of a cozy wedding."

"So did I," Genevieve says. "But these things just get bigger than you can imagine, Emery. Trust me. I know. And you'll want it to be fairy tale perfect, especially since it's your first wedding."

She smiles at Paul again. "And these men of ours, they can try to get stingy if they've already been around the nuptial block. But don't you stand for it, honey!"

Paul doesn't return her smile. He just slices into his steak. I look at Harrison for help, but he clearly isn't paying attention.

"Well, I'll definitely keep that in mind," I say, and then I elbow Harrison. "We both will."

Harrison looks at me confused and nods. Clearly, he has no idea what he's agreeing to.

"They never pay attention," Genevieve says conspiratorially. "But Harrison, your dad and I think a September wedding would be absolutely lovely. Don't you?"

Harrison glances at me and then nods. "September's a good pick."

September? Does this man not know how math works? I'm not going to be waddling down the aisle eight months pregnant!

"Excellent," Genevieve says, turning her attention to her entrée. That's when I notice that hers is a small chicken breast, so small that I'm a little worried about the chicken it came from. Genevieve sees me looking and winks.

"I'm watching my figure," she says. "I bet you are, too,

with the wedding. Did you want me to have them swap you out for this?"

She's still smiling, but her eyes dip to the steak on my plate. There's a small judgment there.

Or maybe a warning.

Is this going to be my life? Watching my figure and worrying about what will happen if I don't stay "cute as a button"? Is that how it works if you want to keep the position of Wife Number Two and fend off the possibility of Wife Number Three?

Not that I have a choice. This baby's going to do a lot more damage than this steak would.

Besides, Harrison isn't anything like his dad.

Unfortunately, just as I think that, I look over and see them take a bite of their food…completely in sync.

I'm screwed.

CHAPTER FOURTEEN

HARRISON

I CAN TELL that lunch took a toll on Emery, but the jury's out on whether it's pregnancy-related or Duke-related. My dad, after all, isn't exactly the world's most welcoming host. He used to be more charming, and he can still tap into it when he needs to, but ever since he retired, he's gotten quieter and less charming. It's as though his introvert tendencies have completely taken over, leaving him grumpy and sullen.

Sometimes, I wonder if he married Genevieve so that she could do all of the talking and leave him to his observing and his people-watching. But the indifferent way he reacted to Emery doesn't sit right with me, so after lunch, I let Genevieve lead Emery off to look at the horses and I corner my dad in his office.

His office is frozen in time, a relic of the sixties with lots of leather, mahogany, hardcover books, and a roaring fireplace. He might've allowed Genevieve to renovate the rest of the house into a magazine-worthy palace, but here, in his cave, it's completely Paul Duke, right down to the fountain pens.

One of those pens is racing across a page right now. He might be retired, but it doesn't mean he's stopped working completely. He still advises the board of his company, and his word's still the law when it comes to major decisions. I don't think he'll ever walk away entirely.

"Working's what makes a man," he told me when I was younger, back when he first gave me that shitty old car to restore. "Build something, son. It'll make you into the person you're meant to be."

Is it true? I look at Duke Capital and what I've built, and pride doesn't begin to cover it. But my company was making Forbes lists even when I was married to Blythe, and I didn't feel satisfied. I didn't feel like I cared about why I was building an empire, just that it needed to be built. Now, with Emery in the picture, with children in the future, it's all different. More rewarding, because of her.

It's something Dad wouldn't understand. I look at my dad and Genevieve, and I know he's never pretended to love her. She's like a very expensive pet, like one of his Derby-winning horses. But she's smart and connected, and she makes his life easy. Maybe, for Dad, that's love.

But he needs to understand that this is different. That Emery's part of my life now, and she deserves respect.

"Dad," I say. "I wanted to talk to you."

He looks at me over his books. He's put on his glasses and looks older than he did at lunch. It's why he refuses to wear them in front of people, I know. He thinks that people will see him wearing his glasses and think he's weak and frail, even if that doesn't make any logical sense.

He doesn't answer me right away, but instead, he watches me expectantly, waiting for me to continue on my own. I pour myself a brandy from the bar cart and then take a seat in the leather armchair across from him. I sip it and watch him, waiting for him to respond to me.

"A poor negotiator will fill the space," Dad would always tell me. "Wait them out, son. Make them answer your questions."

As if remembering what he taught me, Dad chuckles.

"Well played," he says. "I see you haven't forgotten my lessons."

I smile. "How could I?"

He nods, gesturing to the brandy. I get up and pour him a glass and when I pass it to him, he swirls it in his hand as he watches me.

"So," he says. "You're getting married."

I nod.

"Again," he says.

"Seems to be the family tradition," I say. "But Emery's different."

Dad raises an eyebrow. "What makes you so sure?"

"I love her," I say simply.

Dad stares at me, and then he barks out a laugh. Then, realizing that I'm not joking, he straightens up in his chair.

"I love her," I repeat. "And I want you to treat her accordingly. Be nice to her. Make her feel welcome."

Dad looks like I've asked him to leave his fortune to the horses outside.

"I'm not saying give her bear hugs or anything," I say. "Just a little more friendliness. She's from Kansas. She's used to a little more warmth."

Dad shifts in his desk. "You're awfully demanding, aren't you?"

I smirk. "I learned from the best."

Dad considers me. He drains his brandy and smacks it on the table. He tries to wait me out, but I know better. I just watch him until, at last, he knits his fingers together and nods.

"I'll be nicer to the girl," he says. "But son? If you love her, make it stick."

———

I FIND Emery out by the stalls, petting the neck of a sleek chestnut thoroughbred out in the training ring. She sees me coming and turns with a full smile.

"Isn't he beautiful?" she says. "Though I'm going to have to give him a new name. I can't believe your parents just carried on using those Derby names. I'm thinking Rufus."

"Rufus?" I ask, incredulous. "I hope you're better with baby names than you are with horse names."

She laughs. "Probably not."

Even the horse snorts. She gives his nose a pat.

"Genevieve went on and on about his win," she says. "About how much money he's worth and all of that. Which is nice. But I think…he's just a really sweet horse, you know?"

I nod. I can't imagine Emery giving a single shit about which horse won the Kentucky Derby. For her, it's about the connection. And the newly christened Rufus seems to have definitely connected with Emery, judging on how he's nuzzling up against her shoulder.

"I told my mom about him," she says. "I just Facetimed her so she could see him."

"She can come out whenever you want, you know," I

say. "I'll fly her out. And Candace, too, if you want."

She smiles. "Thank you. That means a lot."

She bites her lip, turning back to Rufus. He flicks his ears toward her.

"I wish I could ride him," she says. "I realized when I got out here that it probably isn't something I should do right now. You know, with the baby."

"Probably not," I agree. "But you know, if you're in the mood for riding, there is another option…"

"Harrison!" Emery says, eyes widening as she laughs. "What a line, player. Did you actually expect that to work?"

I shrug. "Worth a shot, right?"

She rolls her eyes. "You're ridiculous."

I smile. "Only with you. Now, why don't we go check out our room?"

"Ooh, are we staying in your old childhood bedroom?" she asks with a wicked little grin. "Should I expect any posters of half-naked women?"

I laugh.

"Not exactly."

"Dirty magazines stuffed under the mattress?"

"I'm sorry to disappoint you," I respond. "But one thing I can promise that it has…"

"Yeah?"

"A bed."

CHAPTER FIFTEEN

EMERY

HARRISON'S CHILDHOOD bedroom is officially nicer than my entire childhood house.

It's painted in light gray with midcentury modern furniture, including a desk and a giant king size bed. There aren't any posters of ladies in bikinis, but rather, several abstract art pieces tastefully arranged on the walls. My guess is that each of them are worth thousands and thousands of dollars.

There's even a wooden bar cart with gold trimming, stacked completely with expensive bottles, selections of fresh limes and oranges, bottles of bitters, and all the mixing tools. I look at Harrison and raise my eyebrow at the sight of this.

"You had a bar cart in your bedroom?"

"Ah, no," he explains. "That's here because we're guests. I wasn't a ten-year-old running around with a gin and tonic or anything."

"That makes me feel better," I murmur. "But seriously, Harrison. This is...extremely nice."

He shrugs. "It's just a guest room. I don't think anything of mine has been here in well over a decade."

There's something a little sad about that. Sure, my room back home is a bit *too* nostalgic, but Harrison's room… It's almost like he's been erased from it.

"At least they didn't turn it in to a gym," I say. "Isn't that what happens in the movies?"

"They wouldn't need to," Harrison says. "Genevieve's converted one of the guest houses into her own yoga/Pilates studio. There's an instructor standing by at all hours in case she feels 'inspired' to exercise."

I stare at him. "You're kidding."

He just laughs.

Could our worlds be any more different? If I wanted exercise, I rode our horses or went for a run.

Of course, Harrison's got his own gym, too. I shouldn't be that surprised. And his place is just as lux as anything in this house, if not more. But there's something about knowing Harrison that's made his penthouse seem almost normal. Or maybe I'm just kidding myself. Maybe it was easier to think of him as someone who at least, at one point in his life, knew what it was like to do his own laundry. But clearly, this was how he was brought up.

I walk around the room and land on two black-and-white photos. One is of Harrison and his dad, side by side. Harrison's in a cap and gown, clearly at his graduation, and his dad's smiling. It's identical to Harrison's. But somehow, even smiling, they both manage to look insanely serious.

Next to the photo is a picture of an old car. Not like an old retro car, but a crappy old Toyota.

Harrison follows me over.

"I guess Genevieve kept a few things in here to make sure it's still 'my room,'" he says. "God, that car."

"What's the deal with that?"

"My dad had me build that car piece by piece," Harrison says. "He told me I needed to learn how to build something from the ground up. He knew it'd be easy for me to grow up into a spoiled brat, so he saw to it that I knew the value of hard work."

I smile. I like that. He was brought up in a place like this, but it wasn't always easy. He's had to fight a little bit.

I bite my lip and bring my fingertips up to run along his cheek. He turns to look at me, and even if he was joking earlier, there's want clearly spelled out in his eyes.

"So, Toyotas turn you on?" Harrison says, smirking. "Good to know."

I laugh. "Not Toyotas. You. This place could've turned you into a very different person. But instead…you grew into a very incredible man."

My lips find his, and the feral part of me that just wants to devour him roars to life.

But then I pull back.

"No one's going to walk in, right?"

Harrison steps back from me and locks the door.

"Considering I'm an adult and not sixteen anymore, I'd say we're safe."

"Well, in that case…"

This time, when his lips meet mine, there's nothing to stop us. His hands go to my chest, flicking my nipples through the thin fabrics of my shirt and bra. And even though I know that Harrison's locked the door, there's still a naughty little thrill of doing this here, with him. That I'll need to keep it down, lest everyone else in the Duke house hear us. Like a passing maid most likely since this place is huge, but still. I'm embracing the risqué.

Harrison must be reading my mind because his fingers trail down to my skirt, yanking it down before running his thumb in circles over my thigh as he guides me back to the bed. And oh yes, it is a *bed*. A cloud of comforters and covers that I sink back into as Harrison follows me down, kissing my neck as his thumb moves dangerously close to my pussy. Any second now he'll discover just how wet I really am. Because even if he was kidding earlier, even if it was just a line... I do want to ride him. I want to feel all of him inside of me, and if I don't get it soon, I'll scream.

Which I can't do.

Because we're in his childhood home.

"Are you trying to drive me crazy?" I pant out as his thumb barely grazes the sheer lace of my panties.

He smirks. "Oh Emery. I'm only getting started."

My name on his lips sends a shiver through me. With his free hand, he tugs my shirt over my head and swiftly unhooks my bra. I gasp as his lips find my breasts, kissing over the bare flesh before his tongue finds one of my nipples. It spikes hard under the slick sensation of his tongue, and he takes me into his mouth just as he slides one of his fingers under my panties and into my wet pussy.

I gasp out his name as the twin sensations ricochet through me, the circling of his tongue and the pumping of his finger. Then, he adds another finger, hooking it inside of me as he finds that spot that makes my thighs quake under his touch.

I'm already feeling the warmth of an orgasm starting to stir inside of me, but then he backs off, and I whimper at the loss of his touch. But before I can even think, he's replaced that finger with his tongue, flicking it in and out of me, flattening it against me, driving me truly out of my mind.

But I don't want to come this way. Not right now. Right now, I want him inside of me.

I push back on my hands, and he looks up, confused, lips slick and glistening.

"Lie down," I demand, and he arches an eyebrow.

"I want you inside of me," I manage. "Now, Harrison. I can't wait any longer."

His eyes darken, but he obliges me, sliding up so that he's lying on his back. He's still wearing his clothes, so I yank his pants down just enough to free his cock, frantic to see him, to feel him.

I don't wait. I can't help it. I'm a woman driven by hormones and lust. I run my tongue along his cock, and then I pop him into my mouth, sucking generously as I take him deeper and deeper into my throat. He groans, fisting his hands in the bed sheets, and I suck harder, using one hand to tease his balls as I feel them, full and aching for me.

Then, I pull back, running my tongue along him one last time before I crawl forward.

He must know what I'm going to do, and his cock twitches in anticipation. I rise up on my knees, placing one leg on either side of him, positioning that huge, throbbing cock between my thighs, and then I slide down the length of him.

The moan that falls out of my lips is too loud, but I don't care. Nothing can describe the feeling of taking him like this inside of me, of how I get to control just how much of him I get. I rock forward and cry out at the intensity, at the sensation that sends stars to my eyes as the base of his cock strikes against my clit like a perfect match.

"You're so fucking hot," Harrison groans, gripping my ass and guiding me as I rock against him, steadily grinding into him as my tits bounce in the air.

He reaches for them, kneading them between his fingers, rolling my nipples under his thumbs, and it sets me off completely. I come around him so hard, and his name leaves my lips before I can dare to take it back. I feel him come, too, pulsing inside of me, pleasure crashing through both of us in perfect sync.

I collapse on top of him when it's over, breathing hard. I turn to Harrison and find that he's grinning, a big goofy grin that makes me laugh.

"What?" I ask.

"I didn't think you'd take my riding joke seriously," he says.

"It was a good suggestion."

He smirks. "You're setting some awfully high standards for the wedding night, you know."

"Hey, speaking of that," I exhale and raise up on one elbow to stare at him. "I know you know how to math, Mr. CEO. Do you realize how pregnant I'll be in September?"

Judging by the expression that crosses his face, he clearly didn't think this through. He rubs his chin.

"Right," he exhales. "So like...how long do we have before you're visibly showing?"

I sigh. "Six weeks, probably, but no one can plan a wedding in six weeks."

"Ye of little faith. I think it's time you learned exactly

what a wedding planner with an unlimited budget can accomplish."

"So Genevieve says," I say, tapping my fingers on his chest. "I'm surprised you were paying attention. But I don't want a giant wedding at the Eiffel Tower."

"No Eiffel Tower," Harrison agrees. "She'll plan whatever you want. Your dream wedding, Emery. Ask for anything you want."

I flush. That is true. All I'll have to do is tell her what I —we—want, and she'll make it happen. It doesn't have to be an insane party like Genevieve was talking about. But it can be the perfect party for Harrison and me.

I look at him, reaching out to run my hand along his chest.

"Can I tell you a secret?"

"Anything," he brings my hand to his lips, kissing the back of it.

"I've entered some weird stage of pregnancy..." He frowns, his brows already drawing together in concern so I rush on. "In which I have become insatiably interested in sex."

The frown disappears, replaced with a growl, low and hungry, then he flips me onto my back before I can say another word.

CHAPTER SIXTEEN

HARRISON

SOMEHOW, my family didn't completely scare off Emery, and she seems invigorated to be heading back to work. Genevieve forced a few engagement gifts on us before we left, one of which was a delicate gold heart necklace with the words Mrs. Duke engraved onto it. I have to hand it to Genevieve. She's a bit of a steamroller, but she does have a talent for charming and wooing. Emery loved it, and when she slipped it on beneath her blouse this morning she'd been glowing. So much in fact, that it takes us multiple attempts just to get out of the house. But eventually, we have to leave, because she's got a meeting first thing and so do I.

"Ramon and I are going over some new media options for one of our campaigns," she tells me in the car. "And we're looking into some new brands. International. I feel so fancy."

"You are fancy," I tell her, and she grins.

I look over and notice that she's not hiding the ring today. She sees me looking and smiles.

"We told our families," she says. "Besides, it's too pretty to hide."

I grin. That's exactly what I want to hear.

At work, Emery's dying for something sweet. I guess I should count my luck that she's not craving something completely disgusting like pickles dipped in peanut butter. Sweet is something we can fix, and easily, especially now that the morning sickness is gone. So, I have Leo detour on our way to work and I dash inside of Supermoon to grab Emery a chocolate croissant. She moans after the first bite, and I raise an eyebrow at her.

"It sounds like you and the croissant might need a moment alone," I joke, and she laughs.

"You'd understand," she says, "if you were busy making a human being. I don't make the rules."

"Fair enough," I agree.

She keeps popping pieces of croissant into her mouth as we step into the elevator. Little bits of flaky dough fall all around us, but Emery's blissed out on chocolate and doesn't even notice. The doors are about to close on us when a hand is thrown out to stop them. A hand with long, white nails.

Immediately, my insides freeze over. I know that hand.

It's the hand of a snake.

The doors slide back open, and there's Blythe, tossing her hair over her shoulder. She's looking down at her phone, and she's stepped into the elevator before she even looks up. I feel Emery tense next to me, and I slide my hand around her hip and squeeze it.

It must be the physical contact that somehow alerts Blythe to our presence. She sees us and then looks up, and her eyes narrow. But I realize it's not merely the sight of us together that's filled her with rage. It's the ring.

"Oh you have *got* to be kidding me," she says.

Emery glances at me, looking thoroughly horrified. She drops the remainder of her croissant back into the paper bag, hurrying to dust the crumbs off of her pantsuit.

"My, you really are the go-getter aren't you?" Blythe asks, glancing at Emery with practiced disinterest. "I only hired you to seduce him; marrying him is quite the leap."

The woman is evil. Pure evil. I open my mouth to tell her to fucking shut it, but Emery's voice pipes up first.

"Excuse me?" Emery replies, her tone clearly indicating what she thinks of Blythe's dig.

"Congratulations though," Blythe adds, sounding just genuine enough I'd believe it if I didn't know better. Then she adds, "Enjoy being the second wife. I hope you get a good prenup."

"Enough," I cut her off before she can add anything else. Then the elevator dings on our floor, opening up. Blythe glances at the pastry bag in Emery's hand.

"And woman to woman, that certainly won't help," she says, and then she fixes her evil eyes on me. "Anyway, Harrison, we need to talk."

I can feel the rage radiating off of Emery as she sputters, but it doesn't matter, because Blythe's already clicking her heels in the other direction.

"I'll take care of her," I promise Emery, but she's too angry to do anything but glare. I give her cheek a quick kiss and then follow Blythe to her office. I know that when Blythe is in one of these moods, she won't stop. I need to nip this in the bud.

"What the hell was that?" I snap at Blythe as soon as I

step into her office. She's fiddling with papers in her desk and doesn't even look up when I walk in.

"You certainly move fast," she says. "Did the dust from our divorce papers even get a chance to settle before you popped the question?"

"Emery is going to be my wife. You'll do well to keep that in mind when you speak to her. Do you understand me, Blythe?"

She shuts the desk drawer with a whip of her wrist as she looks up to glare at me.

"Oh, I hear you, Harrison," she says. "But I don't think you're listening to *me*. I warned you that if you didn't give me what I wanted I'd make your life hell."

"You got the divorce," I say. "I signed the papers."

"But you're refusing to buy me out of this damn charity," she says. "And you're making my life difficult."

"You mean I'm not letting your shitty boyfriend steal my fucking money," I snap back. "I'm not letting you cheat charities and literally take money from babies. I'm not letting you all go on a rampage and destroy my business."

"You're so dramatic," she says. "But I'm warning you again. Give me the buyout I want, or it's going to get ugly."

"Or what? Your boyfriend will keep trying to poach business from me? I dare him to try again."

Blythe's mouth forms a thin line. I watch as she weighs her next words carefully.

"You're stubborn," she says. "To a fault. It was always a problem in our marriage. Maybe you'll learn how to compromise for round two."

"No, Blythe, the problem with our marriage is that you

fucked my best friend," I say, and then I turn to walk away. "And that won't be a problem this time."

"I wouldn't be so sure," she calls after me. "From my experience, she—"

I don't let her finish the sentence. I let the door shut behind us and ignore the look from her assistant when I stalk away.

How dare she think she has any control over me anymore. I see her threats now for what they are—empty. The tantrums of a spoiled brat. How could I have ever trusted her, let alone thought I was in love with her?

No.

What I had with Blythe was never love.

Manipulation, maybe.

Lust, sure.

But if there's anything that Emery's taught me, it's how blind I was before. How I saw something that looked like what I expected my life to be and signed on the fucking dotted line.

But not anymore.

From now on, I'm going to do whatever it takes to cut Blythe out of my life. To keep her away from Emery.

Because I'll be damned if she's going to cause Emery another moment of grief.

CHAPTER SEVENTEEN

EMERY

DID THAT JUST HAPPEN?

Really? I mean, what a b—

I knew that Blythe would find out eventually.

And I knew that she would say something horrible.

But in my head, I had a witty reply. In every scenario that I ran through, I was able to cut her down to size and remind her that I don't give a shit about what she thinks. I'd tell her that Harrison was mine now, that she threw him away and he was the luckier for it because we were happy. I'd tell her she was lonely and pathetic. I'd come up with a creative string of curse words just for her.

Unfortunately for me, none of those burns came to mind after she rolled her eyes and snarked at me in the elevator.

I know, logically, that she's just jealous. I can even stretch myself to imagine that she must be hurt, in her own way. Harrison finally agreeing to the divorce must have stung in its own way, even if the divorce was completely her fault. To see an ex with their new partner, freshly engaged... I'm able to understand why she lashed out, even if I think it's a bitchy thing to do.

The problem is that she said something I've been thinking myself. It was like she used her demon X-ray vision to see that I *am* feeling worried about being the middle wife, the wife who's only a pit stop the way to the third wife. Genevieve's a third wife. I've been worried about the version of her who could replace me. A perfect third wife who only eats salad and chicken breast and who spends all of her time redecorating and collecting Derby-winning horses that she doesn't even ride.

But I can't let Blythe get into my head. I've decided that I'm not going to be the middle wife. I'm going to be the final wife. The forever wife. I look at the rest of the croissant left in the bag and grimace. I'm not about to stop giving in to my pregnancy cravings, but I do need to get some of my shit back in check. In order to do that, I clearly need to figure out a way to blow off steam *and* keep in shape.

So, after work, I let Harrison know that I'm heading to one of my workout classes. He's working late, and he's much more supportive than he was before. Maybe he gets it, finally, that I need my own outlet. Or maybe he's feeling guilty about Blythe. I do wonder what she said to him earlier, and we haven't exactly had a chance to talk. But he tells me he'll pick me up himself once my class is over, and I like that idea.

Bruce meets me outside the office with my gym bag and then we're off to the workout studio. It feels good to walk in here again, and once I'm changed and in class, I channel all of my rage to every kick, punch, and dance-cardio move. I get myself lost in the rhythm, and for a few minutes, I forget about everything: Blythe, the wedding, being pregnant...everything. It's almost as good as the spa. I'm working so hard that I don't even notice when I nearly barrel into William.

"Oh!" I say, adjusting at the last second. "I didn't even see you come in!"

William chuckles, matching the choreography easily. "I got here late. It's been a while, hasn't it?"

I nod. "Busy at work."

It's not exactly a lie. Busy at work. Busy with life. He doesn't need to know my drama. After all, he's just a gym buddy, one I haven't totally decided to trust again after his weirdness about Harrison from before. Except, I should make that clear.

"Got engaged," I add, and yes, maybe it is a bit of a test.

William looks surprised for a brief second before breaking into an easy grin. "You gave the boyfriend a promotion!"

"I did," I laugh in return, throwing a hard jab to my left as I do.

"Congratulations! Have you set a date?"

He seems genuine, and I'm so damn grateful. Maybe the other day with him was just a fluke. He's clearly feeling bad. Maybe he had Harrison confused for someone else. Or maybe I'm just a terrible judge of character. I thought Blythe was the innocent party in the demise of her marriage and I was wrong. I thought William was the villain in this gym friendship, and it seems I was wrong about that too.

"The first Saturday of February!" I tell him, genuinely excited. "We found an opening somewhere great and we jumped on it." Or, our wedding planner did, because we're in a hurry. Because I'm pregnant. But details.

"Damn. Well done," he says. "Congratulations!"

He breaks with the choreography briefly to offer me a fist bump, and my grin widens. See? This is what I'm talking about. Totally misjudged him. And it's great to have a positive reaction to my news after Blythe's outburst this morning. Never underestimate the impact of a friendly smile.

"You know, my fiancé's coming to pick me up," I say. "So you could meet him today, if you like."

William's eyes widen. "Is he really? Well—"

But then we're getting scolded by the instructor that we're not "in the action," so our conversation's forced to a stop. The entire class is sent spinning around the room as we do burpees and jumps to the wall, and at that point, we're separated completely. But it's fine. I spend the rest of the class sweating out my frustration, and by the end, I could take on the world. Hell, I wish Blythe would magically appear because I've got plenty of words to say to her now.

Of course she doesn't.

Which is fine because I know Harrison's going to be waiting for me outside and telling Blythe off isn't worth my time. I look around for William to properly introduce him, but to my surprise, he's nowhere to be found. In fact, he's completely disappeared.

Weird.

I walk outside and there's Harrison. Even though I'm a sweaty mess, he draws me into a hug and kisses me.

"I'm all gross," I protest, but I'm smiling.

"I don't care," Harrison insists. "I've been waiting all

day to have you to myself again. And to apologize for this morning and my troll of an ex-wife. Let me make it up to you."

I blink at him. "Really? How?"

Is he going to shoot Blythe into space? Because I hear billionaires are going into space quite a lot lately and I'm more than willing to tap into Harrison's billions for a one-way ticket for Blythe.

Harrison smiles. "How do you feel about Paris?"

CHAPTER EIGHTEEN

HARRISON

"PARIS? ARE YOU KIDDING?"

The look on Emery's face is priceless. She's more than shocked. She's absolutely frozen in disbelief.

"We'll have a babymoon," I say. "Before the baby, before the wedding. We'll leave tomorrow, if you want to."

She blinks at me. "A babymoon?"

"What? They're a real thing. I asked Sandy about it, after you left."

"I know babymoons are a real thing," Emery says with a small laugh. "But Paris…"

"You loved being a tourist here in New York," I say, taking her hands. "Why not be a tourist in Paris?"

"*You* want to be a tourist again?"

I smile. "I want to do whatever makes you happy. And honestly, you deserve this. If you're feeling up to it, let's go for it. It won't be just the two of us for much longer."

She thinks about it. "But I won't be able to drink any French wine."

I laugh. "We'll go back for that later. But there are plenty of tourist spots in Paris that involve zero wine."

Her face splits into an enormous grin. "Then yes. Let's do it. A babymoon in Paris sounds wonderful. Just one question…"

"Yes?"

"Can we leave right now?"

————

IF THERE'S one part of my lifestyle that Emery's clearly taken to, it's the private plane. And I don't blame her. I called ahead and had them stock the snack cabinet and fridge with her favorite pregnancy snacks and cravings, and she squeals when she sees them. She spends most of the flight reclining on the bed in back, occasionally flipping through one of the several Paris guidebooks that I brought for her.

"Where'd you say we're staying again?" Emery asks me as we get closer to landing.

"The Hôtel de Crillon," I tell her. "Specifically, the Suite Duc de Crillon."

Emery's eyes go wide. "Ohhhh sounds fancy. And expensive."

"You should know by now that I made an exception for the motel in your hometown."

"Excuse me," she quips, barely managing to hide her smile. "The Pearl Street Guesthouses is the height of sophistication."

I raise a brow in reply and she loses the rein on her grin. "You're going to spoil me," she adds with a shake of her head.

"Yes. Yes, I am. Forever. Starting right now, because it looks like we're about to start our descent."

As soon as we land, Emery's mouth falls open, her face in a permanent state of awe. She gawks at everything, at the cobblestone streets, at the cafes and the stores, the Metro signs and the architecture. Once she sees the hotel, she squeals and grabs my hand and points.

It's infectious, her enthusiasm for the world. I've been to Paris many times for meetings, but it was never anywhere special to me. Another grand place, but a place just the same. But with her, it's transformed.

Or maybe it's that I'm transformed.

We check into the hotel where we're immediately greeted by one of the hotel's butlers. He takes us up to our suite, mentioning as we go that our residence for the next week overlooks the Rue Boissy d'Angla, one of his favorite streets in Paris. His English is immaculate, and I'd think he was a native speaker if it wasn't for his French accent.

"The Crillon family had their own chapel," he tells us. "And some of the original woodwork is still a part of your suite. The rest is at the Met in New York."

Emery looks at me and beams.

"Thank you," I tell him, as he opens the door for us and sets down our bags.

Emery looks around, gaping at the enormous rooms. There's gold everywhere, on the framed art and the side tables, woven into the fabrics on the sofas, holding up the lamps. Emery runs her hand over the smooth tabletop and just sighs.

"It's perfect, Harrison," she says. "Absolutely perfect."

I grin. "You ready to see the sights?"

The rest of the week passes in a blur of buttery croissants, Emery charming me with her poor attempts at French and her wide-eyed enthusiasm. We see everything, from the Louvre to the Eiffel Tower, and all the while, Emery adds to her "travel diary," a little leather notebook that she picked up in the giftshop at the hotel.

"I want to remember everything," she tells me as we sit at a café on one of our last days. "Absolutely everything."

She might need the notebook, but I won't. Just looking at her, watching the way the wind ruffles her dress, as she tucks strands of hair behind her ear, I know I'll never forget this moment. I'll never forget being with her like this before everything changes.

It's startling, just how much I'm not scared of what happens next. Because, as long as Emery's with me, it won't matter. It'll be perfect, just like she is.

"What?"

Her voice breaks me out of my thoughts, and I see her looking at me suspiciously.

"I was just thinking about how beautiful you are," I tell her, tucking another errant hair behind her ear. "And how perfect you are."

She bites her lip. "Well, give me a few months and—"

"No," I tell her, kissing her on the lips before continuing. "You'll always be perfect."

She blushes, but she can't hide her smile.

"Now, you have to admit something," she says. "You love being a tourist."

"I do not."

"Lies," she says. "You're loving this."

"I think this is much nicer than the tourist traps we went to in New York."

"Even Top of the Rock?"

I take her hand and turn it so that I can see her ring.

"That one will have a special place in my heart," I say. "But the others…"

"Just admit it. You loved them."

I look at her. I did love it, but I loved it because of her. Does she understand that? Does she understand that I'll do anything for her?

Just in case she doesn't know, I tell her with a long, appropriately French kiss.

CHAPTER NINETEEN

EMERY

SHOPPING IN PARIS is unlike anything I could have ever imagined.

Part of it is that I'm shopping in Paris with Harrison, and we're greeted at every high-end store like they knew we were coming. Or they're just very, very good at spotting money. When we go into Hermès, they pull out a selection of unreleased Birkin bags for me to choose from, all made of supple leather that is softer than anything I've ever touched. And when I can't decide on one, Harrison buys both without thinking.

Then there's Christian Louboutin, where I leave with dresses that literally just walked the Parisian runway. It's all like some incredible fairy tale, and I've got my perfect prince by my side through it all.

Only he's more than any prince I could have ever imagined. He's power to the rest of the world but softness reserved just for me.

And he's mine.

On our last stop down the Champs-Elysées, I spy a

store called Les Enfantines, and in the window is the most beautiful stroller I've ever seen. It doesn't look real, even. It looks like it was pulled straight out of *Madeline*, made of sleek black with soft satin lining the inside.

I can't help myself. I drift toward the window, my hand absently moving to my stomach. Soon, our baby will be here. I'll be one of those moms pushing their stroller through Central Park, and I want desperately for it to be this stroller.

I keep drifting until I'm inside the most elegant children's store to ever exist. Every store that we've been in so far has been decadently decorated, but this place has charm in every boldly colored painting, every cheery rain slicker outfit, every tiny shoe. But even with all of that, I only have eyes for one thing. In fact, embarrassing as it is, I'm totally just gaping at the stroller. Harrison follows me in, chuckling slightly behind me.

"Voyez-vous quelque chose que vous aimez?"

I whip around to see an elegant French woman wearing a perfectly crisp, tailored navy dress. She's smiling politely, probably wondering why any woman would be looking that intently at a baby stroller. I can't help but blush.

"Oh, I'm sorry," I say. "I was just looking at this stroller."

She smiles from Harrison to me.

She switches to heavily accented English as she asks, "You are American?"

I nod. "Guilty."

She laughs. "I love Americans. My name is Marie. Are you interested in this pram?"

"Yes," I say, reaching out to run my finger along the edge of it. "It's beautiful."

I bite my lip, turning to Harrison. "Is it too big to bring back with us?"

Harrison laughs. "Yes, Emery, I'm sure it'll ft. And even if it didn't, there is this little thing called shipping."

My eyes light up, and so do Marie's. She might be French, but she knows encouragement when she sees it.

"Are you shopping for yourself?" Marie asks. "Or a friend?"

I could kiss her for not assuming I'm pregnant. I already feel swollen, especially next to tiny, petite Marie.

"For me," I say, patting my stomach as I glance at Harrison. "For us."

"Well, you are in luck!" Marie says, clapping her hands together. "We have everything you could ever need right here."

And she's right. She shows us to a display of baby clothes that reaches from the floor to the ceiling, to rows of elegant French baby books, to special creams and cloths and woven baby blankets made of wool from local Parisian sheep. Things far too beautiful for a baby to barf on, but I don't care. It's all so lovely that I don't mind letting Harrison spoil me rotten.

"We have the finest items in all of Paris," Marie tells me proudly. "Our collection is the best in the world, even."

"I believe it," I tell her, and I do. If I could build a nursery out of every item in this store, I would. Even Harrison's impressed by the items, and he even picks out a classic rocking horse, painted beautifully.

"Don't worry," he promises me. "We'll also get the baby a real pony. This is just a starter."

I laugh. "Am I allowed to name the pony?"

He smirks. "As long as it's not named Rufus."

I roll my eyes. "Obviously not. That name's already taken."

Every time I think I've found everything magical in the store, something else pops out. Or, more precisely, Marie finds something else. She's not pushy, but she knows that, clearly, this is her one shot with us. And she intends to make the most of it.

I love it all, but I fall especially hard for the tiniest pink dress, embroidered with delicate white flower petals down the side. It's so precious that it takes my breath away, and I don't even realize that I'm tearing up until Harrison stops next to me and catches my tear with his finger.

"It's just so small," I say.

"It's beautiful," he says. "Why don't you add it to the pile."

I sniff. "But we don't even know if we're having a girl."

He thinks about that, and then he spins me so that we're facing each other. He bends down so that our foreheads touch.

"Then we'll just keep having babies until we get a girl," he says, taking my hands.

That's it. The moment I officially melt. Because I know, for absolute certainty, that Harrison doesn't see me as the middle wife. He sees me as his forever.

Just like I see him.

We have one final night in Hôtel de Crillon, and we're barely through the door when he sweeps me up in his arms and carries me to the bed. His kisses run across my mouth, my neck, my chest. I reach for him frantically, so deeply in need of him that my heart might burst here right in the glow of the starry Paris sky peeking through our window.

He pulls my dress up over my head as I tug off his shirt and pants, and then we make quick and frenzied work of what's left underneath. His body meets mine like his hand met mine earlier, totally and completely together, and I know as our bodies move together in this beautiful, gilded room that nothing, absolutely nothing, could take away the happiness burning inside of me now.

"Harrison," I say, touching his cheek as I turn his face to mine. I want to look into his eyes, and when I do, I'm nearly broken by the raw emotion that I see there.

"This was everything," I tell him. "Thank you."

He kisses me, long and deep, letting his tongue run over mine as we taste each other.

"It's not over yet," he promises. "And for the rest of our lives, I'll make sure it's never over."

He moves inside of me, thrusting deep, holding me against him as pleasure wracks through me. My name tumbles off of his lips as we come together, and I fall asleep tangled up in his arms.

Safe and loved.

Forever.

CHAPTER TWENTY

HARRISON

THE BABYMOON GOES OFF BETTER than I could've expected. Emery's practically floating by the time we get back to New York. We're bringing bits of Paris home with us, too. I made note of everything Emery liked. The soaps and bath oils, famous Parisian scents, breads and cheeses, couture chocolates and exquisite macarons. Anything that might bring a smile to her face and remind her of her time in Paris, I made sure was on the plane with us heading home.

But I haven't played all of my surprises yet.

"What a trip!" Emery declares when we walk back into our penthouse in New York. It still feels strange to acknowledge that, that this place is becoming both of ours. Not that I mind. If anything, sharing it with Emery has helped to erase some of the shitty memories I have of the place. She's added light where I thought there would be shadow forever, just as she has with everything in my life.

"Back to the real world, I guess," she says, taking my hand and pressing close to me.

"But at least our 'real world' is so beautiful already."

I smile, touching my forehead to hers.

"I thought you might be missing Paris a bit," I tell her. "So I had a little something set up for you while we were gone."

She arches an eyebrow as I take her hand and walk her into what used to be a guest bedroom. The one closest to the master suite.

"Now, you can change anything in here," I tell her. "This is just a start."

"Harrison Duke, you're being very mysterious," she says. "Did our babymoon have some sort of...covert purpose?"

I grin. "Not originally. But the time away worked out nicely."

"What worked out, exactly?"

I grin and open the door.

She gasps.

The room's mostly empty save for soft, cream carpet and a woven, light gray bassinet. There's a plush rocking chair in a pale gray fabric to match the bassinet. But it's the murals that I want Emery to see. From every angle, it's a different memory from Paris. From the café where we ate croissants to the Eiffel Tower. All painted in a child-friendly version, in pastels that will inspire sweet dreams, I hope. There's even a stork flying over the Eiffel Tower, carrying a painted bundle of joy.

Our bundle of joy.

"Like I said, if you hate it, we can paint something else over it," I say. "I just wanted to surprise you."

"Never," she whispers, twirling to take it all in as her eyes light up. "It's perfect."

"I've got an interior designer standing by," I tell her. "Or you can put it together yourself. It's up to you. I don't want you to be overwhelmed. And I figured this would be a little reminder of the trip."

She smiles, reaching out to take my hand. "I love it. And I want to be a part of pulling it all together. It's something I always talked to my mom about. She—"

Emery falters, looking down as she fidgets with her dress. I watch her carefully, but she turns to me and smiles.

"It's perfect," she says again. "And I'm excited to put it together."

She presses a kiss to my lips, sweet and soft. My hands wrap around her, pulling her tighter. This need to make her happy seems all-consuming, and even as I kiss her, I'm worried about that look from before. Something in me tells me there's something to fix, but I can't put my finger on what.

We pull apart, and she's still smiling. Then, her phone buzzes, and she pulls it out to check for the notification.

"Oh, I almost forgot," she says. "I've got a doctor's appointment this week. Thursday. Did you…"

She trails off, letting me fill in the rest of the question. Giving me an out if I don't want to go to the appointment. Somehow, she's still unsure. She still doesn't believe that I'm going to be hands on. That I'm not going to outsource fatherhood or phone it in.

"Did I want to come to the appointment?" I ask. "Emery, I want to be there for every appointment. Every birth class. Everything you want to do, I'm there."

Her smile widens, luminous and beautiful. I'll do whatever it takes to keep that smile there.

"You are something, Harrison Duke," she says, snuggling closer.

I can't help it. I stand up a little straighter.

She looks back at the mural.

"All of this is."

———

THE NEXT WEEK passes by in a blur, mostly thanks to the impromptu babymoon we took and all the make-up meetings that must be taken as a result. Sandy keeps me on schedule from the moment I walk into the office each morning until I finally escape for dinner. But I don't mind. At least this time things seem to have run more smoothly in my absence. There are fewer mistakes to dig up. If anything, the staff seemed determined to *not* disappoint me while I was gone.

Hell, maybe the key to business success is to take more vacations so they learn not to disappoint you afterwards. I share this new insight with Ramon, and he laughs.

"Are you saying the key to a good business is to be here less?"

I shrug as we drink our coffee on Thursday morning. "I don't know. I've struggled with delegating. I thought I needed to be a part of every detail. But maybe…"

I hear my father in my head, telling me that a man has to know every part of his business, has to have his hands in everything.

But my father didn't have a hand in everything, did he? Not at home. Not with the parts that he didn't want to contribute to. It's not that he was a bad father. But he wasn't an involved one.

Not the kind I want to be.

"Maybe people can only rise to the occasion if you let them," I say, thinking out loud.

Ramon considers this. "Wise words, boss. I think you're invaluable when you're here, and obviously your word is law, but it's good to give people some space to make mistakes and learn from them. Helps them build their own character."

I nod.

"And," Ramon says, nudging me with his elbow. "It helps you to have a little bit better work-life balance, wouldn't you say?"

I roll my eyes but smile in spite of myself. Just the reminder of the trip, of the way Emery looked in the Parisian sunlight coming in through the window of our hotel room...but I stop myself.

I look back at Ramon. "How'd you learn to be a good father? A good husband?"

"I'm still learning," Ramon says. "Every day. But there are some non-negotiables. Like I've got to be home for family dinner, and I always remember to treat Anita like we're still dating. Buy her flowers when she least expects them kind of thing."

"That easy, huh?" I ask. "Family dinner and flowers?"

Ramon grins. "Your mileage may vary. You've got to figure out what works for you and Emery."

It's not bad advice, but it's advice I've got to mull over. I tip my coffee back as I think about it.

"I guess the one bit of bad news that surfaced while you were gone is that we're still hearing those rumblings about you-know-who," Ramon says. "But like I told you before, he's not going to stop. They're going to keep trying to poach, and we're going to keep winning."

"Ignore it," I say. "Let them talk shit. They can't touch us."

Ramon nods. "And…your ex-wife?"

I think about Blythe's smirk and the way she cut Emery down that day in the elevator. I can't let that happen again. I won't let my past control any more of my future.

"I'm still working on it," I admit, even though I haven't been able to give it my proper focus. Not with Paris and catching up once we were back. And now I need to cut out early for the doctor's appointment.

I check my watch. "I need to head out. Emery and I have an appointment."

"Right," Ramon says. "See you tomorrow, boss."

Outside my office I find Emery chatting with Sandy. She turns to me and those doe eyes sweep over me, sending a hungry shiver down my spine. She's in a soft pink dress that swishes just above her knees, showing off the firm muscle of her legs. If anything, she's gotten even hotter while pregnant, which I didn't think was possible.

"Ready?" she says, batting her long eyelashes at me.

"Absolutely," I tell her, and then I give a nod to Sandy. She watches us leave with the kind of smug satisfaction normally reserved for grandmothers.

As Leo drives us over to the doctor's office, Emery fills me in on her day. She's been a smash hit with the clients, and not just with Pink. She's building a roster that any exec would be proud to have, and she's doing it brick by brick. I can't help but admire her.

"What?" she says, stopping mid-story.

"I'm just listening," I tell her.

"No, you're looking at me weirdly," she says.

"I'm just reminiscing about a good business acquisition I made," I say. "A good personal one, too."

She catches my meaning and laughs. "You're ridiculous, you know that?"

I run my thumb over her palm, relishing how she shivers at my touch.

"Now, this doctor," I say. "Am I going to like the guy?"

"*She* is fabulous," Emery corrects. "And yes, you'll like her."

I've never been a fan of doctors' offices. Sterile white walls and the smell of disinfectant around every corner. Which should be a comforting thing, knowing that they keep everything clean. But instead, I'm just reminded that I have no authority or control. I have no power over what the doctor will tell me, or in this case, what they'll tell Emery. No amount of money, no show of force, nothing is going to change what they see when they look at our baby.

It doesn't help that the waiting room's stuffed with other pregnant women, some alone, some with partners next to them, jittery and nervous. I try to relax so that I'm not like the rest of them, but I jump when the nurse says, "Emery Mills?"

This is it. The meeting of a lifetime.

Emery's hand finds mine and squeezes. "Ready?"

No. "Of course."

She keeps hold of my hand, and I force myself to stand up straight, to walk steadily. I can't let her know that I'm fucking terrified. Hell, I'm not the one who's even being looked at. Emery's the one doing everything. The least I can do is be calm.

But it's harder than I imagined to walk through those

doors. The nurse is friendly enough, casting glances back at me as she tries to assure me that Dr. Gonzalez is one of the best in the business. It should be comforting. But it doesn't change the fact that, once Emery's had her vitals checked and she's wearing a stupid paper gown and sitting on the table, I can't help but thinking how vulnerable she looks.

Because of me. Because—

"Ah, you must be Harrison," a voice says, followed by a woman in a white coat emerging through the door.

"Hi, Dr. Gonzalez," Emery says. "It's good to see you."

"How have you been?" Dr. Gonzalez says, her dark eyes focusing on Emery as she walks into the room.

"No more morning sickness, thank God," Emery says with a laugh, sitting up a bit straighter. "And we took a babymoon. To Paris."

She's grinning, and this brings a small smile to Dr. Gonzalez's lips. She looks at me like, hey, maybe I'm not an asshole. I suddenly have an urge to recite all of the things I've learned from the baby books and the blogs that I've read, just to prove to her that I'm not some lazy rich guy along for the ride here. But that might backfire on me, so I decide to keep it simple.

"It's nice to meet you, Doctor," I say. "Thank you for taking care of my fiancée."

Dr. Gonzalez smiles genuinely now. "My pleasure, Harrison. Now, are we ready to check out this baby?"

Are we? Thankfully, Emery nods, and Dr. Gonzalez steps over to Emery, asking her about swelling and leakage and other questions that seem exceptionally invasive, but of course, they're not. In fact, that it's her job. She's taking care of my wife-to-be.

The future mother of my child.

"Now, for the fun part," Dr. Gonzalez says. "I'm going to use the Doppler monitor so that we can hear the heartbeat."

Emery catches my eyes and smiles. I reach for her hand and step closer to her, and then I watch as Dr. Gonzalez sets up the tool, pointing with her free hand to the screen.

"Ah," Dr. Gonzalez says, and I catch my breath. "Here we are."

And then, there it is, coming into the room like a bolt of lightning.

A heartbeat.

A steady little drum.

It feels like the floor drops out from under me at the sound of it, like nothing before this moment truly mattered. Because the sound is so small but powerful.

And it belongs to my child.

Our child.

"That's..." I say, fumbling for the words. "That's incredible."

Emery's crying, and I realize, my eyes aren't quite dry either. But I don't give a damn. Because my baby's heartbeat is echoing through the room.

Fuck. Who knew this was possible? I'd thought I had been happy back when I married Blythe, happy when I started Duke Capital, happy even when I met Emery, but this. Fuck.

Because the love that I'm feeling right now for Emery and the baby is more wild and more massive than I thought possible. Certainly more than I thought could exist in my crotchety old heart. A heart I was sure was too old and wise for love.

Hell, do people *know* about this? About this feeling? I've got to tell people. I've—

I watch Emery's face as she stares at the screen, and I remember the way her face faltered in the nursery.

Of course.

Emery knows this feeling. She's been feeling it ever since she found out. And she wants her people to feel it with her.

Her people.

I'll fix it the second we leave this office. But for now, I'm going to sit here, basking in this incredible sound.

Holding the hand of the love of my life.

CHAPTER TWENTY-ONE

EMERY

HEARING the baby's heartbeat brings out something in Harrison I never expected. He's completely in awe and, there's no doubt about it, undeniably smitten with impending fatherhood.

How could I have ever thought he wouldn't step up to the plate? That he wouldn't want this? Even if it was unexpected. Harrison's a good man. Looking at him now, I have no idea how I doubted him for even a moment. The way he keeps looking at me, or how he keeps stretching out his hand to touch my belly, like he's already bonding with the baby. It basically turns me into a crying, goofy mess all of the time. I'll wake up in the middle of the night to pee—something I am doing with increased regularity—and find his arm slung over me protectively, cradling me and the baby as close as possible without waking me up.

It's beyond sweet. And then, of course, there's the nursery.

When I stood inside the room that had been hollowed out,

stripped clean of its fancy leather bed frame and sleek night-stands, to find a carefully painted mural and plushly carpeted floor just waiting for our baby, it took my breath away.

Mom loved to tell me about the nursery she put together for me. She and Dad didn't have a ton of money to spare, so a lot of the stuff was hand-me-downs from our neighbors. Someone's crib that their baby had just outgrown. A mobile that needed to be fixed before it was put back up again. Rocking horses and toys, clothes and shoes, all from someone else. But she grabbed cans of paint and sewing needles and went to work on it all. The one thing she splurged on—and now, being in Harrison's life, "splurge" is a bit generous—was a comfortable chair that she found on clearance at one of the big furniture stores in the city. It was a beautiful mauve color, cozy and plush, and she built everything else around it.

"I had to have it," she told me when I pointed it out in pictures. "I knew it was where I'd be spending the most time with you."

My heart tightens. I miss my mom more than I thought I would. When I moved to New York the first time, I missed her, but I was so eager to start my new life that it was a dull ache rather than a sharp pain. But now, with every new day of pregnancy comes a whole bunch of new questions, and I just wish I had her here. FaceTime and text messaging just isn't cutting it.

And then there's the wedding dress shopping. The planner that Harrison hired, a sweet but intense woman named Mindy, is taking care of basically everything, from food to décor to the invitations. Once I gave her my prefer-ences, she took everything and ran with it, and it's been a huge relief not to stress over it. But I still have to try them on. I still have to make the final decision.

Alone.

I could bug Mom. I know she'd come. When I told her about the baby and the wedding, she practically fainted on the phone. I know she's thrilled for me. But she's got a whole life on the farm, and it's always hard for her to leave it behind. Near impossible, really. Farm life never stops. It's 24/7 three hundred and sixty-five days a year. Even in winter, there's still the animals to care for. There aren't very many people she trusts to step in. Asking that of her would be too much, and the cost would be astronomical. I know she'd probably be mortified if I offered for Harrison to pay, even if he is a literal billionaire.

No. That's an awkward conversation that I just don't need to have. Plus, it won't be bad or anything. I get to go to Kleinfeld, which I still can't believe. Mom and I would have *Say Yes to the Dress* marathons almost every week, watching the brides try on their variety of sheath dresses and ball gowns. We threw popcorn at the moms who tried to upstage their daughters and cheered when the bride picked the perfect dress. And now, I get to be one of those brides.

Our wedding planner set up the appointment and she's promised she's sending two "experts" along to help me decide. Whatever that means. Rich people do things differently and I've learned to just roll with it.

I grab a pair of high heels since I read that it's good to bring the shoes that you'll be wearing for the wedding, even though I'm a little worried that my feet are going to swell too much by then and I won't be able to wear heels at all. Dr. Gonzalez assured me that she thinks I'll be fine, but I'm still worried. Honestly, I'm worried that the baby's going to grow from the size of a blueberry to a watermelon overnight, skipping right past all the fruits in between. I'm sure of it. Dr. Gonzalez insists that won't be happening for a few months, but I have my doubts.

Harrison's reading his beloved newspaper when I step out, ready to go to Kleinfeld. He gives me the once-over and grins.

"The wedding planner ensured they know you don't have a budget and they're under strict instructions not to tell you the price of anything."

"What does that mean?" I pause, replaying his words in my head while I frown at him.

"It means you have an unlimited budget and you should pick out whatever you want."

"How?" I stare at him and I know my face is betraying exactly what I'm thinking. "How could I possibly pick out a dress without knowing how much it costs? That's crazy!"

Harrison just laughs. "It's easy. Just pick out your favorite. Or buy two if you can't decide. Whatever you want."

"But how will I know which one I like the best if I can't compare the prices?"

Harrison simply laughs at me as he ushers me to the door. He's way too excited about this dress appointment in my opinion.

"Well, thank you," I say, rolling my eyes even though I'm secretly thrilled. "Wish me luck. Apparently I have two experts meeting me at the shop to ensure I don't pick out anything tragic."

I press up on my tiptoes to kiss him goodbye. When I

pull away, he's definitely looking far too mischievous for his own good. Or my own good, possibly.

"What?" I demand of him, playfully slapping his shoulder. "Did you buy the entire store or something?'

He laughs. "Of course not. It's not for sale. I'm just excited about the idea of you in a wedding gown, becoming my wife. Now hurry up and get to your appointment."

"Okay," I agree, but I give him a pointed look like I'm onto him before giving him another kiss and heading downstairs to meet Bruce. I've got to say, I'm having a hard time remembering what it was like to not have a car waiting for me everywhere, ready to whisk me away. It's not terrible, that's for sure.

Kleinfeld Bridal is on West 20th Street in New York City, luxurious white dresses perfectly displayed in the glass below the elegantly lettered sign. As Bruce opens my door, I feel like I might faint right there on the sidewalk. And for once, it's got nothing to do with being pregnant.

How is this my life? It's impossible, yet here I am.

"Enjoy your day, Ms. Mills," Bruce says, gesturing for me to walk up to the door.

And of course they have a doorman. All the best bridal stores do. I mean, I assume, because I've never been in a bridal store before. All I know is the door flies open before I can even think to reach for the handle, a well-dressed man about Bruce's age grinning as he welcomes me inside.

"Ms. Mills!" he says. "Welcome to Kleinfeld. We've been expecting you."

It's exactly like how it looks on the show, except ten thousand times more surreal. There are tall white columns, angled windows above, chandeliers and lights that reflect down on the plush, blue velvet couches. There's light jazz music playing, and several attendants standing by, ready to assist me with whatever I could wish for.

And the dresses. Oh my God, the dresses.

Lace and gems and satin on the mannequins that stand around the room. Layers and layers of tulle cast in trains behind the dresses. Silver jewels glittering from the bodices of some. I walk like a woman possessed toward an A-line beauty, reaching out to touch the dreamy fabric.

I've just gotten close enough when, suddenly, a face pops up from behind the dress.

"Boo!"

I scream, jumping back, but the scream of shock quickly transforms to absolute hysterical joy.

Because the face behind the mannequin is Mom's.

"Mom!" I squeal, diving into her hug. She clutches me tight, and I'm worried I'm going to start crying. Right in the middle of Kleinfeld.

"How…" I start to say, pulling back from her, and then my eyes widen even more at the sight of a freckled face and a huge grin.

"Candace?!"

Candace nods and jumps out from behind Mom to join in the hug.

"You thought we'd miss this?" Candace asks with a laugh. "No way!"

I'm completely floored. Mom and Candace are here, in Kleinfeld Bridal. But how?

Mom reads the question on my face and smiles.

"Harrison got us here," she explains. "He insisted. Absolutely insisted on taking care of everything so that we could be here. Did you know you can hire people to fill in on a farm in the middle of Kansas? I have no idea how he managed it, but professional farmhands are managing everything while I'm gone."

Mom is beaming. I don't think I've ever seen her this excited and well, relaxed. I'm so overwhelmed that my eyes tear up. Mom wipes one away and pulls me into another hug.

"I wouldn't have missed this for the world, Emery," Mom says, low enough just for me to hear. "Clever, rich fiancé or not. I would never have missed this."

How does she know me so well? And how the hell did I think I'd be able to do this without her?

"Enough of the waterworks," Candace says. "I seem to remember there being champagne?"

Of course there's champagne. Not for me, for obvious reasons, but Candace and Mom sip what I'm sure is the *they're not on a budget* bottle while I have a sparkling water. My personal Kleinfeld consultants, because of course I have more than one, run us through the different options and interview me to get a better sense of my taste, and then, before I know it, I've got ten different dresses to try on.

I've never felt more like a princess in my life. Surrounded by an assortment of every lace and beaded dress a girl could dream of, especially with Mom and Candace fluttering around me adding veils and necklaces. Mom loves the ballgowns while Candace tries to talk me into a mermaid style, but it doesn't matter because trying them on is half the fun. They ooh and ahh at all of them, but it isn't until I get to one with a cinched waist that's covered in beaded pearls with an off-the-shoulder tulle overlay over just the right shoulder that I realize that, yes, this is it.

This is the dress I'm going to get married in.

I know I'm right when I come out of the dressing room and stand in front of the tall mirror with its gilded edges. Mom and Candace gasp behind me, and before I know it, we're all crying—even Candace.

"Now you get to do it," Mom says. "You get to say it."

"What?"

Mom laughs. "Oh, don't tell me all of those marathons were for nothing!"

And I do it. I say yes, but not just to the wedding dress.

I'm saying yes to the life I'm embarking on.

I'm saying yes to marrying the love of my life.

CHAPTER TWENTY-TWO

HARRISON

WHEN EMERY TEXTED me a picture of her surrounded by her Mom and Candace, clutching a sign that says "I said yes to the dress at Kleinfeld Bridal," I know she loved the surprise. The three of them show up an hour or so later and find a delicious lunch laid out, full of some of the finest dishes that my chef has to offer, including fresh lobster tails. I catch her mom looking at the dishes simmering in the kitchen with an open mouth and grin.

"They might not hold a candle to your casserole," I tell her, "but you should still give them a shot."

She laughs, shaking her head. "Thank you, Harrison. For everything."

I nod. "Anything for your daughter."

It seems like she wants to say more, but in the end, she just shakes her head. I don't mind. Sometimes, you don't need words to say what you need to say.

The chef tells us it'll be ready in a few minutes, so Emery takes the extra

time to show her mom and Candace the nursery, which

is now exploding with all the baby stuff we got in Paris. There are boxes and bags of clothes and toys and gadgets spilling out of every corner, but it doesn't faze the ladies one bit.

"Well, we're here for the week," her mom says. "Should be plenty of time to get it all together."

"A week?" Emery's mouth drops and she turns to me in disbelief.

"What?" I ask with a laugh. "You didn't think I was going to let them leave after only one day, did you?"

———

"WE'LL WORK on it while you're at work," Candace offers. "I think we need to add a horse somewhere. Harry, you don't mind, right?"

I cringe at the nickname as Emery snorts behind her hand.

"Not at all," I say. "And Emery, take some time off if you want to."

"Hell no," Emery says. "I've got important meetings this week. Besides, I can do both."

"My little worker bee," Mrs. Mills says, flashing her daughter a grin.

"Though…maybe slipping out early wouldn't be the worst thing," Emery admits, watching as Candace holds up one of the baby dresses from Paris. "Or I could work from home…"

"Whatever you need," I say, just before my phone buzzes with a message from Leo. "But we do have a couple more guests that will be joining for lunch."

Emery's eyes widen. "More people?"

"Just two," I say, tucking my phone back in my pocket. "The doorman is sending them up now."

Emery watches me curiously as she follows out of the nursery and down to the front door. I open the door as a tell-tale squeal that only one human being can make reverberates through the entire room.

"Oh, Emery!" Genevieve says, clicking her high heels across the floor before throwing herself on Emery. Emery hugs her back, looking shocked but pleased.

"I had to come, obviously," she says. "And I want to hear *everything* about your wedding planning so far. I tried to get some details from Mindy, but—"

"Slow down, Ginny," says another voice from the hall. "Let the girl breathe."

I turn and find the stately vision of a woman behind me. A woman whose eyes look just like mine, who carries herself with a grace and elegance that I have always tried to emulate. A perfectionist with a quiet, sharp demeanor. Her hair's gone completely silver, cut in a bob that graces her chin. But she hasn't aged. That, at least, all of my dad's wives seem to be in agreement on.

"Emery," I say, grabbing her hand to extricate her from Genevieve's grasp. "This is my mother. Mom, this is Emery Mills."

Mom walks forward, reaching forward with a delicate hand as she shakes Emery's.

"It's a pleasure to meet you, dear," Mom says. "I'm Clara."

Emery's eyes widen but she immediately softens when my Mom smiles at her.

"It's nice to meet you, Clara," Emery says. "I'm so excited to be marrying your son."

Mom nods, releasing her hand before turning to smile at me. And it tells me one clear thing.

She approves.

———

I EAT lunch with the ladies, listening as Genevieve tells a questionable

reenactment of what happened when we visited her and Dad. She's delighted with Emery's knowledge of horses, and she offers to buy Emery a retired racehorse as a wedding gift, but Emery laughingly declines.

Mom and Mrs. Mills get along, swapping what I can only imagine behind their hands as they smirk and laugh together. Then, once talk of wedding dresses begins, I see that it's my cue to head out.

"I'm having dinner with Ramon," I tell the group. "So I'll leave you ladies to get to know each other."

"Is it a bachelor party?" Candace asks, cocking an eyebrow. "Because if so, this our bachelorette and I'm sure New York has some choice strippers."

Emery chokes on her water.

"Candace," she says. "I'm sort of, you know…pregnant?"

"And surrounded by her mother and mothers-in-law," Mrs. Mills says with a laugh.

"Fine," Candace says. "But we should do something fun. Maybe a rom-com night? We need cake or something—"

"Whatever you want," I say. "Give my fiancée everything she desires, ladies. And Genevieve? Behave."

Genevieve laughs and waves me off.

I step over to Emery, taking her hand as she walks me to the door. I grab my coat and then catch her eyes.

"It's just a dinner," I promise her. "Ramon's wife is visiting her parents with the kids and I thought you'd enjoy a girls' night."

"You sure you're not just saying that because I'm knocked up and you don't want me to feel bad?" Emery asks, smiling shyly.

"Of course not," I say. "I wouldn't have fun without you."

It's true. Besides, I've done this before. The first time around, when Robert was my best man, I'd told him I only wanted a guys' night poker game with cigars and too much scotch and the kind of gigantic burgers I'd never be caught dead eating in public. But, apparently, what Robert heard was "get me the VIP strip club experience with limos after steak and high-stakes tables." Meaning, let's run up Harrison's cards as much as possible. It was the kind of night that left me feeling empty and spent, and not in a good way.

This time, everything is different. In the best possible way. Emery.

Plus, Ramon is a definite improvement in the best friend department. He actually listened when I said I hadn't wanted to do much of anything to mark the end of what I now realize was an awfully meaningless time of my life. He's promised a chill night at his house, since his wife took the kids to her parents' house.

Emery's face brightens. "Well, that'll be great."

"You should have fun, too," I say. "And try to keep Genevieve from drinking too much vodka."

Emery laughs. "We'll see."

I give her one last lingering kiss until we hear some loud whoops from the other room, causing Emery to blush and run back to the dining room. I head over to Ramon's, and we kick back with some street tacos and beer with limes. I've got to admit, life is good.

"I'm happy for you, Harrison," Ramon says when we've polished off three or four tacos a piece, sitting on his sofa. "She's good for you."

I nod. "Everything feels better with her. From my personal life to my professional. I don't know how I was operating without her."

"Honestly?" Ramon says. "You were a machine. But now…"

Ramon glances at a family photo on his wall.

"I'm like a real human being," I finish for him. "And it's so much better."

Ramon nods, clinking his beer bottle against mine.

"Speaking of new directions," he says. "I have some new ideas for the charity after we, you know, take care of the situation."

"Oh yeah?" I say, throwing back the beer. "That sounds like plotting, Ramon."

Ramon laughs. "If you say so, boss."

I take another taco.

"Tell me these new ideas," I say. "After all, the best business always comes from nights like these."

CHAPTER TWENTY-THREE

EMERY

AFTER A GIRLS' night in watching rom-coms new and old, from *Bringing Up Baby* to *Overboard* to *Miss Congeniality*, I feel like I've had the best impromptu girls' weekend that I could've dreamed of. Especially since watching Genevieve and Candace interact might be one of my new top ten entertaining things to watch.

"How is she real?" Candace asks later after we've said good night to Harrison's Mom-Mom and Mom Number Three. "Like, was she made in a lab? She's so…"

"Perky?" I offer with a laugh.

"Both literally and figuratively," Mom says from the kitchen where she's washing dishes, and Candace and I collapse into giggles.

"Mom," I tell her once I recover. "You don't have to do that. There's a whole staff."

Mom puts down one of the dishes. "I'm just not used to that."

"I mean, me neither," I admit. "But it's kinda nice."

Mom nods. "And you clearly haven't lost your work ethic."

"And I never will," I tell her. "I mean, Harrison's one of the hardest working men I know. And he grew up around all of this."

"He's a good guy," Candace agrees. "Now, let me check out the guest rooms in this place."

Candace, Mom, and I spend the rest of the week setting up the nursery and meeting with Mindy about the wedding. It'll be here before I know it, but it all feels a billion times easier with the three of them helping me. And more fun. I manage to also stay on top of my work, but time passes way too fast, and before I know it, Mom and Candace are heading back to Kansas.

"We'll be back before you know it," Mom promises. "We can't wait for the wedding."

And it's true. It's only a few weeks away, and it'll be here before I can even blink. Now, I just have to make sure I can still fit into my fancy new wedding dress. I tell the baby to keep the growing healthy but minimal, but Baby Duke doesn't seem to be listening to me. So, I double up on my efforts at my workout class, giving it my all. I even sign up for some classes just for pregnant folks, and I feel completely silly doing the exercises. But if they help keep me in shape— and if they help me with delivery—then I'm all for it.

I also throw myself completely into work. If I only have a few weeks of completely uninterrupted time to focus on work, then I plan to be the best damn worker this company has ever seen.

Except for Harrison. He seems to be matching my energy, and he's completely rejuvenated after our babymoon. He throws himself into work with an enthusiasm that's both more intense and totally different than before. He brings in massage therapists to help with the employees' stress during lunch, and he makes a point to bring up "work-life balance" at multiple meetings. It's like he's seen that our job's important, but there's more to it. And the passion is intoxicating.

In fact, the only thing Harrison seems to take more seriously than his new attitude at work, is his commitment to me and Baby Duke. That, and providing me with as many orgasms as I can stand.

I'm a lucky, lucky girl.

————

TIME FLIES, and soon enough, the date of the wedding is only days away. Mom and Candace fly back in for the week of the wedding. My brother, of course. In fact, basically every Mills family member or neighbor is invited, including Annie, owner of Harrison's favorite motel in Kansas. It's like the entire town of Cottonwood Falls got flown out for the wedding, and even though I wasn't initially thrilled about a giant soiree, it's comforting to see the the Plaza's Grand Ballroom stacked with friendly Kansas faces in their floral dresses and linen suits during the rehearsal dinner.

Harrison's side of the wedding is also clearly visible. Mom-Mom and Mom Number Three are in their best designer dresses, with Harrison's dad quietly brooding in his finest suit. I relish every time one of the Kansas biddies heads over and talks to him, gently breaking through his hard exterior to get a smile every time.

One thing about my town: small talk is a competitive sport, and we excel.

Dinner is incredible; every detail is perfectly executed thanks to Mindy. The most gorgeous pink and white peonies spill across the tables and the wall, leaving the room smelling like a dream. And this is just the rehearsal. I can't even imagine what tomorrow will be like. I'm convinced I'm in a dream when Harrison taps his glass for a toast.

"I want to say some words about the woman I'm lucky enough to sit beside tonight," he says to the room, eyes sliding to me. "Because she's changed my life."

I blush. Harrison's never been one for long speeches. What's he possibly going to say?

"Sometimes you're lucky enough to meet someone who teaches you to look at the world in a different way," he says. "And that, for me, is the woman I'm lucky enough to be marrying tomorrow. Those of you who know me probably know me as a grump—"

Laughter spills through the room.

"—but if you've seen me tonight, you know that, around this beautiful woman, I'm a changed man," he continues. "In fact, I'm the luckiest man in New York. And Emery, I intend to dedicate the rest of my life making you as happy as you've made me."

I can't help it. I'm definitely crying. I'm not even sure that there's a dry eye in the room. He holds up his glass and toasts to our future, and then he settles down in the chair next to me.

We spend the rest of the night surrounded by the people we love the most. By the time everyone's saying their good nights and heading off to their rooms, it all feels like an impossible dream. I hold Harrison's hand as we walk out of the room, ready to separate one last time.

"Tomorrow," he whispers in my ear as we get to the lobby. "You're mine forever."

"Technicalities." I smile. "Because I already am, Harrison."

He grins. "But it'll be official. And I intend to make the most of the celebration."

He pulls back and wags an eyebrow, then looks around. "You know, we could probably find a spare room…"

I laugh and playfully slap his shoulder. "Absolutely not. You know the rule. Separate beds tonight. Besides, Candace is going to be looking for me. It's our last sleepover."

He sighs and presses a final kiss to my lips.

"Until tomorrow, future wife."

I giggle and let him go. He gives me one final look before he turns and heads for the elevator, leaving me to find Candace.

It doesn't take long to find her. She's at one of the now-empty rehearsal dinner tables, though she's not alone. One of the waiters is seated next to her, and their knees are awfully close to each other.

I clear my throat as I walk up, and she jumps up when she sees me. Then, a mischievous smile curling her lips, she darts over to me and pulls me into a hug.

"I'm going to stay for one more drink," she says quickly. "But honestly, don't wait up for me. I'm really hoping to have a New York fling in a broom closet."

I laugh. Of course she is.

"Get it, girl," I tell her, and then I wink. "I'll see you back in our room."

I leave her to get hers, and then I head across the lobby.

Only, I spot someone I'm not expecting to see crossing the lobby at that very moment.

"William?" I say, calling out across the room. "What are you doing here?"

He stops, eyes widening at the sight of me before his face splits into a smile.

"What a surprise," he says. "I work here! What are you doing here?"

I point behind me at where the rehearsal dinner was. "I'm staying the night before my wedding tomorrow!"

He nods, rubbing his chin. "Good choice of places to stay. Listen, I'm off now, do you want to grab one last smoothie? You can tell me how we did on your rehearsal dinner," he adds playfully.

I consider the offer. It's not like I'm going to be able to sleep any time soon, and Candace is clearly not going to be coming up to gossip and watch bad TV anytime soon, so...

He gestures across the lobby. "There's a twenty-four-hour smoothie bar just around the corner."

Of course there is, I think, already smiling. Only in New York. What could it hurt? Besides I was so nervous during the rehearsal dinner—and distracted talking to everyone—that I didn't even finish my dinner. A fact my stomach reminds me of now. A quick smoothie sounds great, actually.

"Okay," I agree.

"Awesome," he says. "Do you mind if I just grab some stuff from my car real fast?"

I agree and follow him to the elevator, where he

punches the button for the basement. My mind is full of jitters and thoughts of tomorrow, playing each of the faces that I hope Harrison will make when he sees me in my dress. What will he say for his vows? And will everything go off without a hitch like Mindy said? I mean, what if I trip and knock the cake over? I'd probably knock it straight into Harrison, ruining his tux. The thought makes me smile, reminding me of the first time we met, when I ruined his shirt by spilling coffee all over him.

We reach the basement, and it's warm from the exhaust of cars going in and out. I follow him to his car, a black BMW, still distractedly envisioning tomorrow. I'm just imagining the way Harrison's lips will curl at the corners before he kisses me for the first time as Mrs. Duke when William opens the trunk.

It's empty. I turn to look at him, confused, when suddenly, everything goes completely black.

CHAPTER TWENTY-FOUR

HARRISON

THE DAY I MARRIED BLYTHE, I remember sitting in my hotel room, waiting for the hour to arrive. It wasn't like I was thinking about the moment of marrying her or of kissing her for the first time as my wife, the way I feel now about Emery. Instead, the hours before marrying Blythe felt a lot like how I feel when I've been waiting for a contract to come in with fresh ink scrawled across the signature page. It was a feeling of accomplishment that came after the dealing had been done, after all the compromises had been made and bargains had been struck. I'd made sure the other party was aware of all of the stipulations. And now, it was time to celebrate a long-awaited agreement finally inked into reality.

Of course, looking back, maybe that should've been a sign. In business I've never had a client violate their contract as thoroughly as Blythe violated our personal one. It was a shitty "contract," obviously.

But none of it matters now. In fact, I feel a wave of gratitude towards Blythe for imploding our lives together because now, with perspective, I can see how bad it was. How wrong for each other we were.

And it's allowed me to find Emery.

Now, I can understand why people do this. Take the risk. Put their hearts on the line. Because Emery is worth every risk in the world. With Emery, I already feel like I've been molded into a better man, and we haven't even said "I do" yet. This is just the start of the celebration, one that I plan to see a lifetime of.

This celebration, though, promises to be spectacular. Or, at least, that's what Mindy kept telling me last night at the rehearsal dinner. I don't care about a single detail as long as Emery's happy. Her smile was effortless and constant, especially during my toast. I'm not a man prone to long speeches of feeling, but Emery brings out my inner sap. Plus, I wanted her to hear how I felt about her, publicly, in front of our family and friends.

There's something odd about not waking up beside her, though. I've gotten so used to having her in my bed, to being able to roll over and run my hand over her body. Of being able to turn her mouth to mine and kiss her until she wakes up. I imagine she's up now in her room with Candace. The hair and makeup people are probably on their way up to help her get ready. Not that they could make her an iota more beautiful than she already is, but she deserves the pampering and I'm glad she's getting the full bridal experience.

I need to start getting ready, too, but it won't take me long. Emery wanted to keep it simple, just Candace as her maid of honor and Ramon as my best man and whatever she wanted was fine with me. All I care about is her greeting me at the end of the aisle.

There's a knock on my door, and I open it to find Ramon bearing coffee and one of his demon children. I guess I shouldn't think of them as terrors anymore. They're just kids filled with kid energy. So I give Cesar a smile and wave them in.

"Cesar wants you to know that he's been practicing," Ramon says, passing the coffee to me. "He's determined to be the best ring-bearer in the history of weddings."

"I don't doubt it," I say, laughing as Cesar does an incredibly serious practice run of walking down the aisle through the hotel room. He's so focused that he doesn't even have time to barrel into me. I almost miss the sensation. Is the kid actually growing on me, or did hearing my own baby's heartbeat turn me into a sentimental softie?

"Well," Ramon says. "Should we get ready?"

The tuxes are brought up, freshly pressed, including a smaller one for Cesar. And God help me—the kid is cute in a mini-suit. I watch how he mimics Ramon's actions, tucking his shirt into his pants the same way, straightening his back, checking his reflection in the mirror. He even tries to tie his own tie around his neck, but it ends up just a mess of fabric. The kid charges over and hands it to me, and then looks at me expectantly.

"Can you help me tie this, please? Make it like Daddy's?"

Shit. I don't know how to tie a kid's tie. I didn't even know how to speak to children using appropriate child-friendly words. I look at Ramon, but one glance tells me he's not helping me. And, honestly, I've got to start figuring out how to do this. Before I know it, my own kid will be here.

"All right," I tell him, getting down on one knee so that we're eye to eye. "Knowing how to tie a tie is an essential part of being an adult, especially a man in the business world. And that's what you want to be, right? Like your dad?"

Cesar frowns at me, like being a businessman is the dumbest suggestion he's ever heard. "I want to be a fire-fighter."

"Well, firefighters need to know this, too," I say, quickly adapting. "They have... balls. I think. So I want you to listen carefully while I show you, okay?"

I've got a flashback to my own dad, showing me how the silk fabric gets flipped and then knotted together to form a perfectly crisp tie.

"Don't be one of those men who can't tie their own damn tie, Harrison," Dad told me. "A real man is self-sufficient. If you find out you've got a meeting in ten minutes, you put the tie on. Do you understand?"

I hadn't. I was maybe ten. But I still got what Dad was saying. I needed to rely on myself. Though I've since learned that maybe a little bit of leaning on others is okay. Teach them so that they can do it themselves, and then give them that chance. Half Dad's lesson, half my own.

It takes Cesar a few tries to get it, but once he does, his face lights up. He keeps showing his dad how to do it and even helps Ramon fix his own. Then, he returns to prac-ticing for his ring-bearer job.

We're watching him do another lap when there's a knock at the door.

I open it to see Candace. She's in a soft blush gown

with her hair pushed back with pearls. She looks at me and grins.

"All right, all right, you guys are super adorable, but I need her back to get ready," she says. "I even got ready on my own to give you two lovebirds a little more time. But we're down to the wire now, so this is the last chance you get to see the bride!"

I stare at her. What is she talking about?

She cranes her head in past me to look at the room. She sees Ramon and Cesar.

She frowns.

"Seriously, Harry. Where is she?"

"Not here," I say, opening the door further to show her, a very uneasy feeling filling my gut. "We weren't sneaking around. Although now I'm sorry I didn't think of it earlier."

"Well then, where is she?"

"Did you check the restaurant?" I ask her, my mind whirling trying to make sense of why Emery would be missing on the morning of our wedding. "She probably needed to eat before she gets nauseous. Pregnancy hunger, you know."

Candace turns pale under her light coating of freckles. "I got in this morning and she wasn't there and the bed wasn't slept in, so I thought she was with you. I went and had breakfast with her mom to give you guys more time."

It takes a moment for the words to hit me completely. Emery hasn't been with her all morning. And she wasn't there last night. Which doesn't make sense since I thought they were having a final sleepover.

"Where were—" I start, and then I shake my head. "Not important. When did you see her last?"

Candace gulps. "Same time you did. At the rehearsal dinner."

But that's impossible. Where would Emery be if not in this hotel? Unless...

Unless she doesn't want to be with me.

Unless she had second thoughts.

Was it all too good to be true? Did Emery get cold feet and realize that I'm not the man for her? That I'm far too stuffy to be the kind of father she wants for our child? That I'm too much of a workaholic for what she wants in a husband? Is she already back on her way to Kansas?

I steel myself for the confirmation.

"Did she say anything?" I ask Candace, not able to look her in the eyes. "Did she say that she didn't want to go through with...with it?"

I can't bring myself to say "she didn't want to go through with marrying me," but Candace must read the heartbreak on my face. She places a hand on my shoulder, her voice softening.

"Harrison. *All* she wants is to marry you. I promise."

Warmth and terror flood through me at the same time. If Emery didn't leave on her own, then...

I'm on the phone before Candace can say another word. Bruce answers almost immediately.

"Did you drive Emery home last night?" I demand.

"No, sir," Bruce says. "Why? Is something wrong?"

"Check everywhere," I tell him. "Check at home, check at her damn gym, her old apartment, check everywhere."

"Of course, sir," Bruce says, and the line goes dead.

I turn from Candace to Ramon, both of them frozen. But it's Candace's face that terrifies me the most.

"Harrison," she says, her voice a knife through the air.

"She would never have left on her own. Never. Which means…"

I don't want her to finish that sentence.

But she doesn't have to.

I know how it ends.

It means that someone took my bride.

CHAPTER TWENTY-FIVE

EMERY

AS SOMEONE who grew up with horses, I've been thrown plenty of times. A horse will spook because of a squirrel running up a tree or a truck starting in the distance, or maybe they've simply got a nervous disposition to begin with. But the point is, that I've had a horse buck and send me flying into the air. The first time it happened, I was eight, and I blacked out from the fear or the impact or both. I woke up to my mom standing above me, a water bottle in her hand and a terrified look on her face.

Dad was there, too. I could see him hovering behind her, unsure of what to do. Mom was always the woman of action, the person who took control. She hissed something to my dad, but he didn't move. He kept watching me as my eyes fluttered fully open, and even though I couldn't make him out clearly, I recognized that he was scared to lose me.

"Are you okay, baby?" Mom had asked. "That was a hard fall."

"Where's Juniper?" I'd asked.

Juniper was the horse who had thrown me. She was my favorite, a white mare speckled with gray spots. She was always sweet and gentle and loved when I gave her carrots. I knew it wasn't her fault that she had been scared, and my first thought was whether or not she was okay.

Mom exchanged a look with Dad, and matching crooked smiles crept on both their faces.

"She's just like you," Dad had said with a laugh. "Worried for the animal first, then herself."

"Juniper's fine," Mom says. "We think it was a snake that spooked her. But she's okay. You're the one we're worried about, love."

Mom had helped me sit up and had given me water. My head was throbbing, and I pressed the heel of my hand to my head.

"You did good," Mom told me. "Your fall, I mean. You rolled off exactly like I taught you. Does it hurt?"

"My head and my shoulder," I said.

"Well, it's good that the head hurts," Mom said. "It's when there's no pain that there's a problem. Still, let's get you home for some rest, ice, and lemonade, how about that?"

From then on, whenever I took a hard tumble off of a horse, that was the cure for the fall: rest, ice, and lemonade. It's why I wake up now with my throat parched and a sharp craving for Mom's sugar-loaded lemonade, finished off with a sprig of lavender.

But there's no Mom or lemonade in sight. Just the headache.

And this fall—was it a fall?—wasn't from a horse. I know that the second I wake up. Something happened that knocked me out last night, but I don't know what. At least,

I think it was last night. How long have I been out? And where...where am I?

Not a hospital. I know that immediately. I've been going to the doctor enough recently that I would recognize the antiseptic smell. No, this is...a room. A small, dark room. I can hear cars outside, but everything's nearly pitched black. I can only make out some overturned desks and chairs and some equipment stacked nearby. I go to move, to sit up, and that's when I realize that there are ropes binding my arms.

Panic stirs inside of me. Who tied my arms? I try to run through my memories, searching for anything that would give me a hint about what the hell's going on right now, forcing myself to breathe and remain calm. I take stock of every ache and pain. The baby. I think I'm okay.

Now how did I get here?

It was my rehearsal dinner. Harrison kissed me good night. Candace went to hook up with the waiter. I walked through the lobby, and that's when I ran into...

William.

The door across from me opens, revealing the bastard in question. He's holding a bottle of water, and rage immediately spills over me.

"What did you *do*?"

William's face, so easygoing and charming in our cardio class, looks, for a moment, like it normally does. His eyes even bulge a little, like he's innocent in all of this and has no idea how I got here with my ropes.

But then his face changes. It darkens, eyes narrowing, a full evil sneer crossing his face.

"Me?" William basically snarls. "Nothing. The question is, what did your *fiancé* do?"

"Harrison didn't do this to me."

He would never hurt me. Or our baby. I know this for a fact, though I'm not certain it's wise to say this out loud, though. Not with the way William's looking at me, like he's been waiting for this moment for a long, long time.

William smirks as if he can read my mind. I shift against my bindings, but it's no use. They're tied so tight that a sharp end of the rope cuts into my wrist.

"Oh he did, when he decided to ruin lives left and right," William says, pacing in front of me. He sets the water on a table nearby, too far out of reach for me to get to. Seeing it out of reach makes me realize how parched I am right now. And how vulnerable I am.

William keeps pacing, his voice getting progressively louder as he unleashes the monologue he's clearly been holding on to for a while.

"It was only a matter of time before someone wasn't content to just roll over and let him take and take and take!"

His last word is a shout, and suddenly, I'm more terrified than ever. Clearly, William's been holding in his crazy for long enough that it's explosive now. And anger this explosive… Will he hurt me?

The baby.

I have to think about the baby. I have to do whatever it takes to keep William calm so I can get out of this alive.

"He'll give you whatever you want right now," I tell him, trying to keep the fear out of my voice. "Right now. Call him! My phone's in my purse—"

William barks out a harsh laugh. "You really think I'm that stupid? Your purse is in a dumpster behind the hotel."

Shit. Wherever I am, Harrison won't be able to trace my phone. He'll go to find me, and…

Oh God.

Our wedding.

The hotel.

Today's supposed to be my wedding day.

This prick kidnapped me and now I'm missing my own damn wedding?

Will Harrison think—will he think I ran? Will he even be looking for me?

"It's okay, just call the company, call Duke, they'll put you through," I say, still trying to sound as calm as I can. "He'll do whatever you want. He'll pay you whatever you ask."

William stops pacing, facing the dark wall away from me. When he speaks, his tone has dropped to a cold, emotionless growl.

"He's going to pay all right."

I shiver but force myself not to cower in front of this horrible man.

"He'll murder you if anything happens to me," I tell him. "You know that, right?"

William turns, shadows dancing across his eyes.

"I don't have to murder you to make him pay."

CHAPTER TWENTY-SIX

"WHERE THE FUCK is the security footage?"

Never in my life have I felt terrified adrenaline coursing through me like this. All I know is that, until Emery is back, every second will be spent looking for her. And even though everyone's trying to help, it's not enough.

Nothing is enough. Not even close.

At least Mindy is proving herself to be useful. She might be a wedding planner, but something tells me she may have also spent some time in the CIA the way she flies into action the second I tell her that Emery's missing. She flips her dark hair over her shoulder and whips out her iPad.

"I'll have Darren bring us the security footage here directly."

"Is he the manager?" I snap. "Because I've been trying to get an answer from him for ten minutes—"

"Darren's head of security," Mindy says. "Tom's the manager, and he's useless. But once we get the footage, we'll be able to find her, Mr. Duke. Trust me. I've never lost a bride."

I wish it were that simple. But this isn't as simple as a runaway bride.

I wish it were.

I wish Emery had stood me up at the altar rather than been taken against her will. Because I know without a shadow of a doubt that's what's happened. And I'd take her leaving me over being hurt. Always.

Bruce and Leo have already confirmed she didn't go home, or to the office. Now they're checking basically every place in New York Emery has been. Her gym, her old apartment, but I don't expect them to find her in any of those places. Candace ransacks the hotel room she and Emery were supposed to share looking for any kind of clue, but there's nothing. The only thing we learn is that Emery never even opened up her suitcase. She never put on her pajamas or brushed her teeth. Whatever happened, it happened in that lobby.

Which is why we need the damn security footage.

"It'll be okay, Harrison," Ramon says quietly, placing a hand on my shoulder.

The action forces me to stop pacing. I look down, hands shaking. I've been in constant motion ever since Candace arrived looking for Emery.

My eyes cut to Ramon's.

"I appreciate you, Ramon, I do," I say. "But you don't know that. Right now, she could be hurt. So please don't tell me she's okay until it's a confirmed fact."

I don't say it to be an asshole, but it comes out that way anyway. But Ramon doesn't look hurt or annoyed. He simply nods.

"Darren's team found something," Mindy announces, tapping the headpiece she's wearing.

I rush over to her, opening my mouth to demand what she knows, but she holds up a hand as she listens.

"Right," she says into her headpiece. "Bring it up here, anyway."

She catches my eye and says, "They found her purse in the dumpster."

My heart sinks. Emery's purse in a dumpster. No one's saying it, that it's a terrible sign, but I feel it. But I can't let myself sink into despair. Despair is a place I won't come back from, and that won't do shit for Emery.

"Shouldn't we be calling the police?" Candace asks.

"Darren did," Mindy says. "They're on their way."

I make other calls to anyone and everyone I can, anyone who seems like they might know. But most of the people Emery would go to are here. Her mom. Her brother. Her old roommates.

Thankfully, Mindy's pull with Darren seems to be strong enough that he shows up shortly with the footage. He's a serious man, no frills, no wasted words. He gets right to it with his team of three, having them hook up the feed to play through my hotel TV in minutes. There, I can see all the different camera feeds of The Plaza being shuffled through in quick succession.

"Last seen around nine p.m. in the lobby, correct?" Darren asks, flipping through the video feeds with impressive speed.

"Yes," I confirm. "We were staying in separate rooms last night. I left her in the lobby around nine. I assumed she was headed straight for her room."

"It's my fault," Candace wails, pacing nearly as much as I am. "If I hadn't—"

"It's not your fault," I manage to mutter, mostly so she'll shut up. My focus is on the video feeds.

"It is," Candace says firmly. "She's my best friend, and —there she is!"

Candace jumps forward, pointing at the TV screen as Darren slams the button to stop the footage.

There, in the lobby, is Emery. She's standing in front of me, though I'm hard to make out because of the position of the camera. But not her. She's beautiful. Perfectly radiant, even in the grainy camera footage, in the dress she wore for last night's rehearsal dinner. I watch as she sees me leave, and then she turns and heads off-screen.

"She came back to talk to me," Candace says. "And...I told her I'd be out late. I never should've left her alone!"

"You couldn't have known," I say, and even though it's true, there's still a pang of irritation going through me. What if Candace had stayed?

Emery reemerges in the lobby, and then she must see someone else off-screen because she appears to be smiling and calling out to someone.

"Who's coming over to talk to her?" Candace asks, trying to get closer to the screen.

Darren squints at the screen. "Looks like a man. I can only see half of him. Do any of you recognize him?"

Mindy, Candace, and I all shake our heads.

"It's impossible to make him out with this angle," Darren says. "She seems like she knows him, though."

Knows him? From where?

"They're heading to the elevator," he says. "Perfect. We have cameras in the elevators."

Darren switches over the footage to the elevator. Emery gets in, and now, she's more visible than ever. She doesn't look worried. In fact, she looks...wistful? Dreamy?

Thinking of our wedding, I think. *Where she should be right now.*

"He knows where the cameras were," Darren says, anger seeping into his voice. "He's purposefully standing so that we don't get a good shot of his face."

I watch as the elevator opens, not on one of the floors, but on concrete.

"The parking garage," Darren explains. "Let me pull up that camera. I'll send someone down there now."

I'm already texting Bruce, who I know is parked there now, waiting for further instructions. I tell him to search it for Emery, and he confirms that he's on it.

"Here's the parking garage feed," Darren says, pointing to where we see Emery and the guy walking. Now, his face is more visible, and he looks familiar. But it's still not clear enough for anything to click.

"They're heading to a car," Darren says. "Black BMW. I'll see if we can zoom in on the license plate—"

But Darren stops talking. He grabs the remote and backs up.

"What?" I say quickly, looking from Darren to the screen. "What did you see?"

Darren doesn't meet my eyes. He continues to watch the screen. After rewinding, he presses play. I watch closely, trying to see what he sees.

The man stands next to Emery as he opens the trunk. Then, he puts his arm around her shoulder.

Jealousy spikes hard and fast inside of me, and I nearly punch the wall. But before I can, the video continues.

Emery sags into the man's arms and he dumps her into his trunk.

Blind rage.

I'm not sure I'm even breathing when Darren replays the sequence on a slower speed.

"I think he might have drugged her," he says, pointing at the screen. "She's walking and alert until this moment," he says, pointing at the screen. "She's limp and unconscious when he places her in the trunk."

I'm silent, still processing the nightmare this footage has revealed. That was over twelve hours ago. Emery has been missing all night. Drugged. Dumped in a trunk.

Darren speaks into his own headpiece, his voice sharp and clipped, giving directions about updating the police, running the plates. Beyond that, I don't hear anything. I think Mindy or maybe Candace or maybe both of them grab me and take me to the bathroom, where they force me to grip both sides of the sink as I breathe. All I can hear is white noise roaring in my head, my brain playing the sight of Emery being dropped into a trunk like cargo over and over.

Emery, who should be dressing for our wedding right now.

Emery, pregnant with our baby.

I scream in frustration, slamming my fist against the porcelain as I send tiny soaps and shampoos flying off of the sink.

It's fog and blackness for the next several minutes until, thankfully, someone calls Darren with the plate info. I watch as Darren scribbles down a name into his notebook. Then, he turns to me.

"We've got an owner on the car," Darren says. "Does the name Robert Dyson mean anything to you?"

This time, I don't almost punch a wall.

I do.

And it cracks under my fist as I unleash a stream of the worst curses known to man.

――――

I HAVE HATED Robert more than seemed possible for the past year. At times, it's been such a powerful and potent hatred that I occasionally questioned whether or not he could have really deserved it. Then, I would remember the sight of him with Blythe, naked, and how he smirked at me every time after. And I knew the hatred was well-placed.

But this?

Kidnapping and endangering my pregnant fiancée? It seems unspeakably low, even for him. Beyond even his weaselly tendencies.

I don't hear the voices of anyone behind me as I leave the room. Nothing registers as I jab the elevator button, my fingers furiously tapping out a text to tell Leo to meet me out front. I don't even wait for his response before I stuff my phone back into my pocket.

"Harrison!" Candace's voice echoes behind me. "Wait a damn second!"

I stop with my hand on the open elevator door to look back at her. She's out of breath running after me, with Mindy and Darren in tow.

"Send that footage to my phone," I say to Darren.

"Candace, stay here and get her family together. Make sure they're all right. I'll be back with Emery. I promise."

"Harrison—"

"I know this man," I tell Candace. "He's the man who fucked me over and stole my first wife. And I won't let him hurt Emery."

"Is he dangerous?" Candace asks, her eyes clouding over.

No. I never would have thought so. Sneaky, conniving, sure. But not a fucking kidnapper.

"I'm going to get her back," I say instead. "Trust me."

"I'm coming with you," this is from Ramon, who has joined the trio in the hallway wanting answers.

"It's Robert," I tell him, barely managing to get the words out.

Ramon doesn't wait for an invitation, he simply pushes past the group and onto the elevator.

I don't bother arguing. I just release the elevator doors while jabbing the button for the lobby.

"The footage," I remind Darren as the doors slide shut. "Send it."

CHAPTER TWENTY-SEVEN

HARRISON

AS SOON AS Leo slows the car in front of Robert's address, I explode out of the vehicle. I move so quickly that it's like everything around me doesn't exist. I barely register Ramon next to me, who's trying to tell me to calm down, telling me to think before acting. All I see is the door, which I raise my fist and pound on.

It swings open almost immediately, revealing the bastard himself. He has the goddamn nerve to smirk at the sight of me.

"What did you *do*?!" I roar, giving him the smallest second of time to answer before my fist meets his face.

There's the satisfying crack of his nose as he goes down with a groan. I'm about to jump on him, to beat him sense-less, but Ramon's arms are around me before I can. In the background, I hear Leo shouting at me.

"For fuck's sake," comes a voice from inside the house. "Aren't you supposed to be married by now, not obsessing over me?"

It's enough to make me pause. I look up and see Blythe

wide-eyed, still in her damn silk pajamas. Were she and Robert in on this together? Was I really married to someone capable of this? I barely resist the urge to lunge at her.

"Don't you dare talk about her," I snarl at Blythe. "Especially not now."

"What the fuck are you talking about, Harrison?" Blythe snaps, reaching down to help Robert off the ground. I don't want to let her since the asshole deserves to stay on the ground, but Ramon holds me back. Robert wipes the blood seeping out of his nose on his shirt sleeve.

"Emery," I say, practically breathing fire. "I'm talking about the fact that Emery was drugged and tossed into Robert's trunk last night."

"Stop it," Blythe says dismissively, but her pulse has increased and her eyes are wide.

I hand her my phone, the footage that Darren sent me already playing on the screen.

Blythe blinks at me suspiciously, then leans forward to examine the footage. "Robert was with me all night," she murmurs.

"That's right," Robert snaps, still wiping his nose with his sleeve.

"So it couldn't have been—wait," Blythe cuts herself off. "Hang on, Robert. Look at this."

But Robert doesn't look. He tilts his head back pinching his nose like a fucking bitch. Behind me, Ramon hands me a handkerchief that I pass begrudgingly to Robert.

"What is it, Blythe?" I ask.

"That man," Blythe says, rewinding and pausing the footage. "Robert...it's your brother."

Robert still doesn't look at her. "What does William have to do with anything?"

"It's him," Blythe insists. "It's William on the tape."

Finally, the asshole has the decency to look at the tape. And I realize, even with Robert's fucked-up nose, that his face is exactly where I saw the familiarity.

Robert's eyes meet mine, nothing but dismissive nonchalance in them.

"I don't know," Robert says. "You can barely see him."

"Bullshit," I snap. "Maybe you're not seeing straight. I could punch you again, if it'll help."

"You—"

"Robert, listen to me," Blythe says. "And Harrison, cut the shit. It's not going to help."

She gives me a glare and turns my phone to show it to Robert.

"We both know he's been obsessing again," she says. "Asking all of those questions…"

"What questions?" I ask.

"Uh, should we move this inside?" Ramon says from behind me, nodding at a neighbor walking her dog in our direction.

Robert looks like he wants to say hell no, but Blythe nods and waves us in.

"He's been obsessing," Blythe says again, once Ramon and I are in and the door is shut. "About, well. About you, Harrison."

"Why the hell does he give a shit about me?"

Blythe bites her lip, then lowers her voice. "He blames you. For, you know. What happened with their company."

"Don't bother whispering," I say. "This isn't some

damn office gossip, Blythe. This is my fiancée in the hands of a maniac."

"He's not…" Blythe says, but she trails off, glancing back at the bathroom where the sound of water running emanates. "You remember what happened. They sold the company to you. It was one of your first deals."

"One of the shittiest deals I've ever made," I growl. "They'd basically turned it into a damn Ponzi scheme before they sold it to me. It was nothing but parts."

Blythe glances again over her shoulder. "Right, but they don't see it that way. They see it—especially William —as you ruining their family company."

"Ruined it?" I balk. "I gave every employee proper compensation before I stripped it. And maybe their derelict dad shouldn't have run it into the ground—"

"Harrison," Ramon says, his voice a warning that I need to focus.

"The point is," Blythe says. "William's always talked about wanting to get his 'revenge' on you for profiting off their downfall. It's why he tried to poach Pink."

My eyes widen. "That's why the asshole was coming for me?"

"Exactly," Blythe says. "And I thought—and Robert did too—that he was just going to fuck with your business. But…there's a chance he's a little unbalanced."

I meet Blythe's eyes with a narrowed glare. Unbalanced is an understatement.

Blythe has the decency to blush. She looks away, then back to me, her eyes wide.

"I told him about Emery," she admits. "He knew that I'd hired her to—well, that's not important right now. He knew about her. If she left with him willingly, it's possible he insinuated himself into her life somewhere along the way without any of us realizing. I didn't think he'd *do* anything, really…"

If it weren't against every code of ethics in my body, I might punch Blythe right now.

"He was stalking my fiancée? My *pregnant* fiancée? And no one thought this was a concern?"

Blythe actually does look like she's been punched now, but I don't have time to spare her feelings.

"I didn't know," she insists, and even for Blythe, she looks genuine. "I truly didn't know, Harrison. I had no idea he'd taken his revenge fantasies this far. Or that he'd even be capable of anything like this."

"Where would he take her, Blythe? Does he have an apartment?"

"Not there," she says. "He has roommates. But maybe…"

"Our dad's old warehouse," Robert's voice says from the hall. We look up to see him standing there. "I'll give you the address. But then I want you gone, Harrison."

"You don't get to make that call, Robert," Blythe says, surprising us all before she turns back to me. "But he's right. The warehouse. It's getting demolished in a few days. He'd take her there."

"Then get me that address," I say, standing with Ramon. "And Robert, I promise you, if she's not okay, I'm coming for you next. And I'll break more than your fucking nose."

I don't give him time to respond. Blythe's already texted me the address, and I head outside, straight for the driver's side of the car. Leo's already standing on the pavement, waiting for me. Like he anticipated my next request.

"Leo, stay here and make sure these two don't go anywhere," I say with my voice low.

"Of course, sir," Leo says.

"Have Bruce meet you. Follow them if needed."

Leo nods. "Go get our girl, sir."

I smile for the first time today at the use of "our." Emery charms every life she touches.

"I will, Leo."

"Harrison?" It's Blythe, still standing on the porch in her pajamas, looking lost. "I'm sorry." I look at her for a moment, seeing the weight of everything she's apologizing for written on her face. The thing is, that's her burden now, not mine. I nod at her.

"Me too."

Then, Ramon and I are in the car, and we're gone.

Hoping to all hell that we're not too late.

CHAPTER TWENTY-EIGHT

EMERY

I WAS NEVER a huge *Dateline* person, but I would watch it whenever Mom had it on. And I learned some things. Things I never thought I would actually need to know, but today—tonight?—I'm grateful.

The big thing I learned from *Dateline* was that it's important to humanize yourself. You can't just be the random person they kidnapped. You have to humanize yourself and relate to them, even in a small way, so that they won't hurt you.

Of course, before, I thought that William cared about me as a friend. I thought he was my dance-cardio buddy. Did I think he was a little jilted and maybe jealous of Harrison? Obviously. But I thought that meant he was a regular, semi-douchey guy. Not a kidnapper.

Now that I see that he is a kidnapper—one fixated on my soon-to-be husband—I need to figure out a way to not, as he so ominously put it "make him pay" using me. Which means I need to bust out my Kansas charm.

I look around, trying to find some talking points.

Unfortunately, I'm able to think of absolutely nothing. I assume this place must be some kind of warehouse. There's some spare furniture in the form of overturned desks and tables, a few chairs, and an old couch that's had the cushions slashed. None of it seems like something light and humanizing.

I tell myself it's not hopeless, though. Eventually he let me go to the bathroom. It was the equivalent of a gas station bathroom with a tiny toilet and a sink. Unfortunately, the water wasn't working, but I managed not to gag. But the real win came when I left the bathroom. He handed me a water bottle and then didn't tie me back up to the chair. He looked distracted by his phone. So maybe he's starting to make mistakes. Or he's just super forgetful. Whatever it is, I'm taking it.

"So, where'd you grow up?" I ask him, sitting on my hands so that he doesn't see them and remember he needs to tie me up.

He glances over at me. He's sitting on one of the chairs, scrolling through his phone. If only I could get my hands on that phone and call Harrison.

"What does it matter where I grew up?" William asks me. "Before, you never cared. All you wanted to do was talk about your idiot fiancé."

Ouch. Harsh but true. Not the idiot part, but he's right. I suppose I didn't ask much about him. Still, I don't give into the bait.

"I grew up in Kansas," I tell him. "Tiny little town. Learned how to ride horses before I could walk. No, really. Mom has a picture of me on her chest in one of those baby slings with her seated on a horse when I was a baby. Couldn't walk, but I could ride."

William just stares at me. I take a breath and continue.

"It's a really small town," I say. "So small that it makes you wonder if the rest of the world really exists. Every place you go, there's someone that's known you since you were little. Everyone knows your business. I loved it, but I also knew I wanted something more, you know? I didn't want to lose out on the chance of who I could be. Of who I wanted to be."

I wait for him to react to this statement, but he doesn't. He just keeps staring at me like everything I'm saying is irrelevant.

I throw on a smile and pretend to be undeterred, as if we're just two friends having coffee rather than a kidnapper and his kidnappee.

"Do you have kids?" I ask, hoping for an in for some sympathy as a pregnant woman.

"No," he says. "I hate kids."

Whelp. There goes that as leverage.

"Well, you know, sometimes, people change their minds," I say. "I didn't know if I wanted kids. But now that I'm having one—"

"I wouldn't have kids even if I wanted them," he snaps. "What would I give them? What shit legacy could I pass down?"

Now, it's my turn to stare. What is he talking about?

"Don't tell me your shitty fiancé never told you about how he really got rich," William snipes. "How he went and stole other family businesses, ground them up into dust, and left the families that built them on the streets to starve."

He slams his fist on the table next to him, causing it to teeter on its weak legs.

"I should've inherited an empire," he says. "But I didn't. Because of fucking Harrison Duke. And what do I get instead? Nothing. I'm broke, living on nothing while that asshole gets to live the life I should be living."

Some of this feels like a stretch. For one, William lives in Manhattan. I'm pretty sure he showed up in designer sneakers and sweats on more than one occasion to our dance classes. He's not living on nothing, clearly. But what matters is that he's talking to me. He's talking, and we're bonding.

Sort of.

"I know what it's like to have to rearrange your expectations for life," I admit. "My dad fucked up and cheated on my mom. Which would have been terrible on its own, you know, realizing your family was a lie. But then he left me and my mom with so much debt, and you know what great life he left us for? A life with his dental hygienist. Isn't that just the pits? I got my job at Duke to help pay off all of those bills. Help my mom save the farm."

William rolls his eyes. "Yes, and fucking the boss certainly helped your bottom line."

I ignore that comment. "The point is, I made a choice not to wallow. I decided that I'd be the one to turn stuff around for us. I wasn't going to make my dad's poor choice—"

"My dad never made a 'poor choice,'" William growls. "The only poor choice he made was to trust Harrison."

"As I was saying," I say. "I chose to make a change and to do something positive. And you can, too. You can—"

CRASH!

There's a sound like a car barreling through the side of the building.

No.

Not like the sound of a car.

There actually *is* a car that's crashed into the building.

And there, sitting in the driver's seat, is my fiancé, Harrison Duke.

CHAPTER TWENTY-NINE

SUBTLETY HAS NEVER BEEN my style. Not as a businessman. Not as a boyfriend. And apparently, not as a man
who's fighting to get his fiancée freed by a madman.

As soon as we get to the warehouse, it's clear that the
front door of the warehouse isn't an option. In fact, it isn't
even clear where the door should be. The entire front of
the warehouse has been boarded up and painted over with
black paint. There's no way of telling what's inside.

Which is exactly how I knew that we found the place
where William's stashed Emery.

"He might be in there with her," Ramon warned me
when we did our first circle of the place. "He might be
using her as bait to get to you."

"No," I said. "There's no 'maybe.' That's clearly his
plan. Don't you see the cameras?"

I pointed them out as we did another lap down the
street, trying to keep the circling as inconspicuous as
possible.

Ramon checked them out. "You're right. Cameras on

an abandoned warehouse? Either they're worried about squatters, or…"

"Or he's watching to see when I get there," I said. "Probably on his phone. So we need to head in there in a way that's unexpected."

"Or," Ramon offered. "We wait for the cops to show up. You did text them when we left, right?"

"I texted Darren," I say. "But I'm not waiting. Every second we waste waiting—we have no idea what he's capable of."

"So then how are we getting in?" Ramon had asked.

I was grateful he didn't argue with me or try to stop me. It was another reason for why he made a great friend and best man, even though this was, I'm sure, the last thing he would've ever thought of as one of his duties for today.

But this also might put the man in danger, and knowing him as a friend and a family man, I wasn't about to let him go any further.

"Get out of the car," I told him.

"What?" Ramon asked, looking confused.

"I'm about to do something stupid," I told him. "And you shouldn't be in the car when I do it."

I idled the car on the street at an angle from the warehouse, nodding in the direction of the building.

His eyes bulged. "Harrison, you're not serious."

"It's the fastest way to get inside. And my entire life is in that building."

I saw the doubt flash across Ramon's face.

"The building is boarded up. All I need to do is take out enough of the boards so we can gain entry. But I need you to get out of the car in case this plan is shit. Keep an eye on the building in case William makes a run for it. Direct the police when they get here."

He must have realized there was no talking me out of it, because he opened the door and stepped out of the car. And then he met my eyes. "Be careful," he implored before shutting the door.

"Cross the street," I told him. "And wait for the cops."

I watched him cross, careful to angle his body away from the cameras, not that William would recognize him anyway.

Then, there was nothing to do. Nothing except floor it.

And sideswipe into the warehouse.

———

THE CAR DOES EXACTLY what I want it to do, breaking down the side of the building. The airbags deploy, of course. It stunned me for a moment, but my adrenaline is running so high I'm out of the car a moment later.

I see Emery immediately, relief flooding through me that she's okay. She's alive. She's cowering in a chair, shock on her face, but she's okay.

———

"WHAT THE FUCK?" William roars. I'd laugh if I wasn't planning on killing him. He's pissed I broke up his kidnapping? Fuck him.

"What the hell did you think you were doing, William?" I shout, looking around as I take in the space. Disgusting run-down warehouse in exactly the condition you'd expect of something about to be demolished.

In response, a bullet ricochets off of something to my left. A near miss meant for me, I'm sure. I drop to the ground, rage coursing through me. This isn't over. This lunatic has a gun and if Emery ends up in the crossfire, I will never forgive myself.

"Emery!" I shout, turning back to where I saw her last, reassuring myself that she's not between me and this madman.

"He's over there!" Emery shouts back, nodding in the other direction. "He's—"

Whizz!

Another bullet, but this one flies right over Emery's head and she screams. She rocks back so hard on the chair that she tips it over, and then she crashes down to the ground.

"Emery!"

Whizz!

"Those were warning shots, Harrison!" William shouts out. "Get any closer to her, and I swear to God, I'll shoot her. How would that feel, Harrison? Entire damn legacy down the drain?"

I'm roiling with rage now. I whip my head back and forth, and finally, I see him, crouched behind an over-turned table. I lose all sense of myself and sprint head-on for the table, thinking of only one thing: beating this asshole to a pulp.

"Harrison, no!"

I keep running. William's going to have to stand if he wants a clear shot of me. And when he does, I'll tackle him to the ground.

I'm running hard, straight for him, and according to plan, he stands up.

Only I misjudged the distance and him, because there's the gun.

Pointed straight at my chest.

And then Emery is sprinting out of the corner, straight towards William.

"*No!*"

The roar is mine this time. But she doesn't stop. William turns his head in her direction, but she's already too close. She's already reached her destination. A metal shelving unit to Williams right, which she barrels into with enough force to send it crashing onto William before he even realizes what's happening.

In the flurry of falling metal, his gun clatters to the ground. I reach down and grab it, pointing it straight at William who's already struggling to crawl free of the mess.

"He's not worth it, Harrison," Emery says, her voice thick with disgust.

"She's right," says a voice behind me, and I turn to see Ramon and a police officer stepping through the impromptu door that I created with my car.

I turn the gun over to the officer, never taking my eyes off the bastard.

"Arrest him," I snarl. "This asshole tried to kill my fiancée."

"You would've deserved it," William gasps out, finally freeing himself of the wreckage. He's unarmed and the police have a gun on him, so I'm not terribly concerned. "You and that little—"

Emery walks over and interrupts his tirade with a swift kick in the balls. He groans at the force of it, immediately silenced.

"You shut your mouth," she snaps at him. "You shut your mouth about my fiancé, you prick!"

I stare at her, in awe. And in spite of everything I'm nearly tempted to laugh at her feisty defense of me to a madman. So relieved that neither of us is dead. But also, what if William had turned the gun on her? She never should have put herself in danger trying to save me. I'm the reason she's in this mess to begin with.

She meets my gaze, and my worries must be written all over my face because she's already shaking her head, about to turn her sass on me, it would seem.

"You did not think I was just going to sit by and let him shoot you, did you?"

"I can't believe you just did that," I say, waving in the general direction of the shelving disaster.

"I'm a very clever problem solver," she says, tossing back her hair.

"No, being very clever would've been running," I say. "You could've been killed."

"I wasn't the one running straight at the bad guy," she reminds me, watching as the officer frees William from the metal only to immediately lock him in handcuffs. She watches with narrowed eyes as they walk him away.

"I'm allowed to do that," I say. "You do crazy things when you're in love, after all."

She smiles at me, pulling me closer as she buries her face in my chest.

"You're okay?" I ask, setting her back to scan her from head to toe.

"I'm okay," she reassures me. "You're stuck with me forever."

I grin. "That was the point of getting married, you know."

"I missed my own wedding."

I shrug. "We'll reschedule it."

"Nope," she slaps my chest. "We. Will. Not. Today is our wedding day, Harrison Duke, and I intend to hold you to that. You promised me that wedding planner could make anything I wanted, happen. Let's make this happen."

I stare at her. "You aren't serious. You've just been kidnapped. Tossed in a trunk and tied up in a warehouse all night and nearly shot."

"Exactly," she says. "So you should give me what I want, shouldn't you? Are you in or out, Mr. Duke?"

Hell. She already knows the answer. Whatever she wants, I would be in no matter what.

"I'm in," I agree. "But this is the last time I let you have your way"—she raises a brow at that before I can continue—"until you're officially Mrs. Duke."

She grins.

CHAPTER THIRTY

EMERY

WHEN I CALL MINDY, her first question is whether or not I'm okay. And after I assure her I am, her next question is to ask the first question again, because I've just updated her on my plans for the rest of the day.

"You want to reschedule the wedding for...today?" she asks, I suppose not quite believing her ears.

"Today," I confirm. "You're the best, Mindy. I know you can pull this off."

"Damn right I can," Mindy agrees, and I think I hear a little bit of glee in her voice. As if she appreciates the challenge. "This isn't the first time I've had to audible a wedding due to a missing bride, even if it is my first missing bride due to a kidnapping."

I'm intrigued about how many "audibles" Mindy's had that involved brides not showing up on time but she doesn't give me a chance to ask.

"We've still got all the flowers," she charges on. "And the cake. I've got your dress and Harrison's got his tux, of course. We rented the ballroom all night so—"

"Change of venue," I interrupt to tell her.

"Oh? I'm intrigued."

"I want to surprise Harrison," I tell her, shooting a sideways glance at the man himself with a grin. "So I'll text you what I have in mind."

True to everything I've been promised about Mindy, she simply promises she'll make it happen and we hang up.

―――――

NEXT, we head home, and Harrison and I have one final rendezvous as technically-single-people in the shower before people start arriving to help us get ready. Candace is the first one there with my dress.

"So," Harrison says while Candace does my makeup. "Where is this mysterious new wedding venue?"

I wink at him in the mirror. "Oh, you're going to love it."

"Right," he says. "But you do know I'm not leaving you alone before we get there, right?"

I stick my tongue out at him. "You'll see the dress if you don't. And that's bad luck."

He watches me. For a guy that's been worried about me taking the subway alone, today wasn't easy for him. But I need him to know that I'm going to be fine. And I need him to trust me when I tell him that.

He takes a deep breath. "Fine. But Candace?"

Candace looks up from where she's been dusting my cheeks.

"Do not take your eyes off of her until she's standing beside me again, all right?"

Candace salutes him. "You got it, Harry."

Harrison's eyes meet mine, shining and perfect.

"See you there, Ms. Mills."

I smile. "Forever yours, Mr. Duke."

———

I WONDER what Harrison's face looked like when Leo brought him to the office. I'll never know, because even though we've already seen each other today, I'm determined that we won't see each other again until I'm walking down the aisle to become Mrs. Harrison Duke.

Mindy's filled the entire lobby of Duke Capital with the flowers from the ceremony and the reception, meaning there basically isn't a spot to step without running into a beautiful bouquet. It smells like a florist shop.

With a hint of coffee shop.

The memory of that first coffee spill makes me smile. The spill that started it all, the one that destined him to keeping a supply of extra shirts on hand. Because of me. His Coffee Girl.

I wouldn't have it any other way.

Which is what made me realize that this very lobby was the perfect place to make it official. Forever.

Our guest list dwindled a bit with all the chaos of this morning and the relocation, but most of them—the most important ones, at least—are here. Mindy managed to get enough chairs from I don't know where, the woman really is a wedding genie. I'm awed, honestly. The lobby has been transformed into a wonderland, more perfect than The Plaza could've ever been. She's managed to install trees of some kind, ropes of twinkling fairy lights strung from one to the next creating a magical romantic canopy.

"It's time, Emery," Mindy says next to me, just as the song I've been waiting to hear my whole life starts up on the keyboard.

Then, my mom's next to me, waiting to walk me down our makeshift aisle. One look at her and I'm tearing up.

"I'm so proud of you, baby," she says. "For everything."

I know she was terrified today, but I also know that no one could've better raised me to handle myself in the last twenty-four hours. She helped make me the woman I am. She gave me the courage to have big dreams and chase them.

She gave me the foundation, the confidence, I'll need to raise my own children.

"Let's go get that man of yours," Mom says, pressing a kiss to my cheek.

And we walk, stepping through the curtains that Mindy used to keep me and my dress from view.

A sea of smiling faces greet me. Sandy, Ramon, my old roommates, Candace, my brother, and more. But only one face holds my attention.

His.

Eyes burning with a fire just for me. A smile that only brightens when I'm around. My perfect man.

And I get to have him forever.

"I like your choice of venue," he says when I reach him. "Very us."

"This is where we met, after all," I remind him. "This is where I became yours."

"My Coffee Girl."

"Forever."

He doesn't wait. He kisses me, much to the chagrin of our officiant. Cheers and whoops go up from the crowd until, finally, I giggle and pull away.

"Let's make this official," I tell him. "No more delays, even for kisses." And then I take his hands in mine.

He smiles at me and nods. We listen as the officiant asks us to confirm our commitments, as he asks if this is forever, if this is until death do us part.

It is. I've seen his commitment for myself, and he's seen mine.

Harrison saved me, and I saved him right back.

And that, that is how you live happily ever after.

EPILOGUE
HARRISON

"HARRISON, your wife's on her way in," Sandy's voice says through the speaker on my desk. "Along with a couple of stowaways."

Business at Duke Capital's been booming, more successful than even I had ever dreamed of. All around me, I hear the symphony of phones ringing, deals being made. But I also hear the sounds of people on the phone with their partners. I see pictures of children displayed on employee desks. And most importantly, I see the honors and awards that decorate our offices from the local charities that we've supported.

I see the progress of a vision finally coming to fruition, one I could've never foreseen on my own.

The door bangs open, and I can only see the top of a ponytail whipping past my desk. Then, there's Ellie, popping up next to me with eyes that look exactly like her mother's. The mischievous smile isn't too far off, either.

"Daddy!" Ellie squeals, launching herself into my lap.

"Well, well, this is a surprise," I tell her. "And how is my baby girl?"

"I'm a big girl now!" she reminds me, as she's prone to do ever since she was promoted to big sister.

"That you are," I agree. "But you'll always be my baby girl."

"That's silly, Daddy," she sings, patting me on the chest with a chubby hand. A hand that leaves a streak of what appears to be pink frosting.

I pull a wet wipe out of my desk drawer and go to work on her hand without missing a beat.

"Did Mommy give you one of those donuts with pink frosting?"

"Noooo." She shakes her head very seriously, eyes wide.

"Are you sure?"

She nods, still the picture of innocence. "I snuck it," she confesses in a whisper, a sly grin breaking out across her face.

"You," I tell her with as much seriousness as I can muster, tossing the wipe in the trash, "are gonna be trouble." Heaven help me.

"I know, I know!" She grins and claps her hands.

I can't help it. I laugh. Behind Ellie, Emery appears in the doorway, our six-month-old son on her hip. He spots me and squeals with delight, and I set Ellie down so that I can step away from my desk to take him from my wife.

My wife.

My perfect, brilliant, incredible wife. Before she can say a word, I've caught her lips in mine. She tastes like coffee and caramel, delicious and sweet. If only the entire day could be spent kissing her, but Dylan makes his presence known by attempting to strangle me with my tie. The kids got a grip on him.

Emery makes an "mmm" sound against my lips as she pulls back, her doe eyes glittering at me. I know she's thinking the same thing I am. The thing that resulted in these two little rascals in the first place.

"Nanny's sick," she explains. "And I've got a huge day."

"Of course you do," I agree. "You're the hardest working woman I know."

She grins. "I've got a big meeting today with a potential donor for the charity. A Broadway production company. I'm hoping I can convince them into donating theatre space for the fundraiser."

"Which fundraiser?" I ask, smiling because she's got at least a half dozen in progress at any given time.

"The one to fund dance classes for kids in need," Emery says, her enthusiasm clear. "I've got so many ideas for this one, I don't know how I'm going to squeeze them all in."

"How are the donations?"

"Already ahead of my initial projections, so I'm raising the bar."

"Of course you are." I grin.

"This charity would never have gotten off to the right start if they didn't have this platform," Emery gushes. "All that potential, swept under the rug."

"They're lucky they have you as an advocate," I tell her.

"Let's do a horse party!" Ellie pipes up from where she's using highlighter to draw a horse across one of my most recent contracts.

Oh well. Hope the client has kids. Or a sense of humor.

"You know Mommy loves that idea," I say, and I look and see that Emery's already smiling.

"I told her on the way over I have a meeting next week with a charity that needs money for their horses. It's a therapeutic riding program," she adds.

"Sounds great," I tell her, bouncing Dylan in my arms.

"Daddy, I want up, too!" Ellie says, launching herself at me and promptly dumping half her sippy cup down my shirt.

"Some things never change," I say, grinning at Emery as I set Ellie down.

Emery's already fishing for a clean shirt out of my drawer. She chucks it to me and takes Dylan back momentarily while I shrug off the old shirt, relishing the way Emery's eyes rake across my chest. The moment's pretty PG with Ellie making airplane noises in the background, but as a new parent, I take what I can get.

"I've got two new interns starting this week too," Emery says. "I've got so many balls in the air, I cannot wait to delegate a bit of it and hear all their ideas. I can't do it all myself."

Emery's managed to overhaul the charity wing of Duke Capital into a force to be reckoned with. She does more good in a week than most people do in a lifetime. Truly, the woman never ceases to amaze me.

"Really?" I say. "Could've fooled me. You make it look easy."

"Do I?"

"Hmm," I say, watching Emery's mouth quirk and wanting so badly to kiss her again. "Be careful with the interns, though. They tend to spill stuff."

"Oh, really?" Emery says, acting faux-surprised. "That sounds like a problem."

I smirk, pulling her against me once more.

"It does, doesn't it? Unless it turns out that you have a fetish for having coffee spilled on you."

"What a very specific fetish, Mr. Duke." My wife grins. "I guess you got lucky then."

"There's no doubt about that, Mrs. Duke."

PAIGE PRESS

Paige Press isn't just Laurelin Paige anymore...

Laurelin Paige has expanded her publishing company to bring readers even more hot romances.

Sign up for our newsletter to get the latest news about our releases and receive a free book from one of our amazing authors:

Laurelin Paige
Stella Gray
CD Reiss
Jenna Scott
Raven Jayne
JD Hawkins
Poppy Dunne
Lia Hunt

ALSO BY LIA HUNT

The Billionaire's Intern Trilogy

The Billionaire's Intern

The Billionaire's Mistake

The Billionaire's Promise

ABOUT THE AUTHOR

Lia Hunt is a pen name for two writers who adore billion-aires and virgins with scorching love scenes, jaw-dropping cliffhangers, and swoony happy endings.

Made in the USA
Coppell, TX
17 July 2022

80093796R00132